LEIA'S PLAYMAKER

A Curvy Girl Hockey Romance

Nichole Rose

Nichole Rose

CONTENTS

DEDICATION

To the fierce women who refuse to be tamed. You're amazing.

ABOUT THE BOOK

The last thing this curvy girl expected to find in the locker room in the middle of a game? A grumpy, naked hockey hunk.

Colter Bayliss

Fighting during a game is bound to happen.

Getting ejected for instigating?

That's a whole different situation.

But here I am anyway...banished to the locker room for a series of fights I didn't even start.

Imagine my surprise when a curvy little goddess waltzes in and sees everything (and I do mean everything).

Leia Marsh has the smartest mouth and sassiest smile I've ever seen.

She swears she got lost, but I know a thing or two about trouble.

And this little spitfire has it written all over her.

She's up to something, and I intend to find out what.

As soon as I do, I'm marrying her.

Leia Marsh

When your bestie thinks her new boyfriend might be a bookie, you do a little digging.

Which is precisely how I ended up in the Falcons' locker room.

I didn't expect to find Colter Bayliss naked.

Nor did I expect the crazy hockey player to be so bossy.

Now, I can't seem to get him out of my hair.

He's determined to solve this mystery with me.

And the more time I spend with him, the less I want to solve it alone.

But can I trust Colter with my heart, or am I just something to help him pass the time?

CHAPTER ONE

Leia

Excited fans pack the arena, decked out in team colors to support the Silver Spoon Falcons—the new AHL team—at their second home game of the season. The action on the ice moves too quickly for me to keep up. I don't know much about hockey, but it seems very...hands on.

One of the guys on our team—Number 88—has already been in two fights. He won both from what I could see. He doesn't like Bruce Gordon on the Stingrays much. Not that I blame him. Bruce has been harassing him the entire game. At least, that's what it looks like to me and everyone except the referees.

Bruce is up to no good.

"Are you kidding me?" The old man sitting closest to where I'm standing jumps to his feet with the rest of the crowd, shouting as Bruce collides with Number 88 again. "Learn to skate, you dirty rascal!"

I bite my tongue, trying not to laugh as the old man shakes a fist at the ice in fury.

Maybe I should go to games more often if they're all this crazy.

I snort at the thought. Unless I find what I came looking for tonight, I may be coming to more games anyway. I just graduated with a degree in journalism and moved to Silver Spoon Falls. My roommate and friend, Elysa, is dating a new guy, Gavin Cochran. He claims he's into investing. She's convinced he's involved in illegal gambling. I thought she was just being dramatic, but I agreed to investigate anyway to appease her.

I did not expect to find Gavin meeting with Jimmy Brinks from the Timberwolves last week when they were in town. I chalked it up to coincidence until I also caught him meeting with Bruce Gordon behind the arena before the game tonight. This time, I managed to get pictures of Gavin handing Bruce a fat wad of cash.

They're in cahoots. I'm just not sure what they're plotting. I thought maybe Gavin was paying them to throw games, but the Timberwolves won last week. And Bruce isn't playing to lose now. But what does that leave?

My brother is the athlete in our family. I know nothing about sports or sports betting or why a bookie would pay a player when one solitary player can't guarantee a win.

I'd very much like to know, though.

Play resumes on the ice and the crowd settles down. I scoot closer to the exit leading toward the player area. Thanks to my job at the local paper, I have a press pass, but it doesn't grant me a whole lot of access. Not the kind I need, anyway. I intend to do a little snooping in the Stingrays' locker room while they're on the ice.

Number 88 gains control of the puck and takes off down the ice with it. As the crowd leaps to their feet, I slip through the exit into the back hallway, holding my breath. Security must be preoccupied by the game because they don't yell after me.

I exhale a tiny breath and take stock of my surroundings. The hallway is a wide passage made of concrete blocks and cement with fluorescent lights overhead. There's only one direction to go, so I shrug and follow the path. It slopes downward.

I grumble and walk slowly. Maybe heels weren't a good idea.

At the bottom of the steep slope, the hallway branches in three directions. I have no idea which way to go from here. I peer down the hall to the left and right, but it curves in each direction several yards ahead, blocking my view. I take the hallway directly ahead—the one where I can see doors branching off on each side.

I peer into the first but can't tell what's inside. Jiggling the handle is useless. It's locked.

I huff and move onto the second. It's a storeroom for the concession stands. Boxes of food supplies line the metal shelves. The third is some sort of boiler room. The fourth is a janitor's closet. Mops, buckets, brooms, and one of those industrial-sized floor waxers are crammed into the tight space. It smells like bleach.

"Good job, Leia. You picked the wrong hallway," I mutter in disgust. Where's Charlie when I need her?

"Yo, Tony! Grab more Bud Light while you're down there."

"Crap!" I slip into the janitor's closet, pressing my back up against the wall.

"Yeah, yeah," Tony shouts back from the end of the hall. "I've got it."

I definitely should have brought Charlie with me on this mission. My younger sister causes as many problems as she solves, but when it comes to sneaking around, she's got a lot more experience than I do. She's been bluffing her way out of one predicament or another her whole life.

Me? Not so much.

My smart mouth is liable to sink me deeper before it gets me out of trouble. I don't like being told what to do. Or where to go. Or what I can or can't know.

I press my ear to the door, straining to hear Tony moving around in the storeroom two doors down. Sound doesn't carry through the concrete well. I can't hear anything. I give up trying and wait a full five minutes before carefully poking my head out.

The coast is clear.

I scurry back down the hallway and turn right.

Breathe, Leia. Breathe.

I force myself to slow my steps slightly and stand up straight. If you act like you're supposed to be there, most people don't question you as much. Since I have a press pass, hopefully if I run into anyone, they'll just assume I'm where I'm supposed to be.

Forty-five seconds later, I get to test that theory. I round the corner, and a row of doors come into view, alongside a security guard playing on his cell phone. He's leaning against the wall not even five feet from a set of double doors. It must be a locker room.

He flicks his gaze up at me.

"Hello." I give him a polite, confident smile.

He eyes me silently, his brows furrowing.

Crap. He's going to stop me.

I pick up the pace, veering toward the door.

"You can't go in—"

"I'm with the press." I flash him my badge and scurry through the doors before he has a chance to say a word. The doors swing shut behind me.

I inhale a relieved breath...and let it out in a shocked rush. This isn't the Stingrays' locker room. The giant emblem on the carpet in the middle of the room is a falcon, and the locker room is decked out in blue and white. I think a bomb went off at some point. Benches are overturned. Pads have been flung across the floor. There's even a pair of pants dangling from the edge of a locker.

"What the fuck?"

I spin to the left with my hand over my heart.

Holy crap.

Number 88 looked like a beast on the ice. It's nothing compared to the sight of him standing in front of me wearing nothing but tattoos and a dark scowl. He is...wow. Yes. That's it, exactly. He is wow. He's a good six-four with the body of an athlete. Makes sense, all things considered.

"Where did you come from?" I gape, caught completely off-guard by the sight of him.

"Where did I come from?" He flicks his gaze up and down my body. His hazel eyes linger a little bit longer than they should on my chest. "Shouldn't I be the one asking you that?"

Oh, right.

"Got lost," I lie. "You were on the ice ten minutes ago. How are you naked now?" I peel my gaze away from his ridiculous body—I bet being God's favorite is seriously awesome—and scan the locker room. "And what happened in here? A freaking tornado?"

"Again with the questions?"

"I like to know things." I turn back to him, my gaze naturally falling to his...Good grief. Why is it hard? "Can you please put away your..." I wave my hand in the general direction of his dick. "That monster?"

"Uh, no?" He quirks a brow. "You snuck into our locker room. If you didn't want to see my dick, you shouldn't have followed me. And if you don't want him to be hard, you should stop talking."

I scowl at him, which makes him shrug, completely unrepentant. So I refuse to acknowledge the last part of his statement. I don't even know what the last part of his statement *means*. "I did not follow you. I thought you were still on the ice where you're supposed to be," I protest. "And you still haven't explained why you aren't there, by the way."

"Got ejected from the game." He scowls, reaching up to touch his finger to his lip. Only then do I notice that it's split. There's a small cut above his right eyebrow too, partially hidden by the damp blond strands plastered to his head. "For instigating. The ref decided he had enough of me *attacking* Gordon."

I snort. "Maybe if the ref got his head out of Bruce Gordon's butt, he could clearly see that Gordon started those fights."

Number 88's scowl slips. His eyes crinkle at the corner as his lips curve into a grin. He's got a pirate's smile, the kind that screams trouble. The kind that makes my stomach flutter. "At least we agree on that much," he says, taking a step toward me. His erection bobs, drawing my attention again.

Jeez. It's even harder now. I thought dicks were supposed to be ugly, but his is kind of beautiful. Or maybe I've officially lost my mind. Who am I kidding? I'm standing in a locker room with a naked hockey player, grilling him about why he's in the locker room as if I have a right. I've definitely lost my mind.

"You're staring at my cock again, goddess."

"I am not!" I squeak, wheeling around so quickly my head spins.

"I'll let you look all you want if you tell me your name."

"Leia."

He chuckles and I press my hands to my overheated cheeks.

"I did *not* give you my name because I want to look at your junk," I growl. "I need a favor."

"Did you just insult my dick?"

"What? No. Oh my gosh. Why are we even talking about it?" I cry. How is this happening right now? My sisters are never going to let me live this down when they find out.

"You're the one who keeps bringing him up." He chuckles. "In more ways than one."

"Oh, my God. Stop talking!"

He laughs again. "What kind of favor do you need, Trouble?"

"What's your name?"

"My name is your favor?"

"No," I groan and close my eyes. "This would go so much faster if you'd put clothes on so I can look at you."

"Again, no. How do you not know my name, but you know that fucker's name?" he growls.

"Who?"

"Bruce Gordon."

"Long story."

"I've got time."

"Well, I don't. And I don't know anything about hockey."

"But you know Bruce Gordon."

"I know his *name*. If you'd quit being irritating, I'd know yours too."

"Colter Bayliss."

"Colter," I repeat, resisting the urge to shiver as I say it. It fits him, though I'm not sure why.

"Say my name again and you'll be naked in this locker room too, Leia."

I whip around to face him. Only he isn't across the room anymore. He's standing right in front of me. So freaking close I practically bump into him. He grasps my arms to keep me from tipping over backward. His scent wraps around me and my entire body quivers. I brush against his erection in the process.

"Fuck," he mutters, his pupils flaring as he sways toward me. His jaw turns to granite as he tries to get himself in check.

"Let me go," I whisper, my whole body aching for something that it shouldn't want. I don't even know this man. Just because he's naked and touching me shouldn't make me want to jump into his arms. And yet...that's exactly what I want to do.

"Tell me why you're in our locker room."

"I got lost."

"Who were you trying to surprise?" His gaze rakes across my face, his expression hard.

"Who was I trying to...?" My stomach sinks as realization dawns. I jerk out of his hold, putting space between us. He thinks I'm a puck bunny. "I'm not a puck bunny, Colter. I'm a journalist. I'm looking into a story and got lost. That's it."

"What story?"

"One that doesn't involve you."

"What story, Leia?"

"One about a bossy hockey player who gets ejected from games and destroys locker rooms," I snap, rolling my eyes. Until he accused me of being a puck bunny, I fully intended to recruit him to help me. But now? No thanks. "Is that what you want to hear? That I'm writing a story about you? Well, too bad because I'm not. My story has nothing to do with you or your giant ego."

He narrows his eyes at me, growling softly. "I like that smart fucking mouth, Trouble. The more you sass me with it, the more I want to fill it."

"Too bad for you because I'm not a puck bunny." I poke him in the chest. "And another thing, buster, I don't even *like* hockey!"

He throws his head back and laughs.

I consider punching him in the throat, and then decide I probably shouldn't. He's already been in more than enough fights tonight. Besides, violence never solves anything. At least that's what Adalynn, my older sister, keeps telling me.

I decide she's probably right. Instead of punching him, I just growl at him and stomp toward the doors.

He grabs me before I make it two steps, hauling me up against his chest. His lips touch the side of my throat. "I'm going to find out what you're up to, Trouble. Don't think I won't."

"Well, good luck with that because I'm not going to make it easy for you, Bossy."

His rough hands glide across my chest, sending waves of heat through me.

My core clenches. I fight the urge to whimper, refusing to fall under his spell. He's grumpy and bossy and I'm not entirely sure I even like him all that much.

Liar, liar, pants on fire, a little voice whispers.

I imagine myself smothering it with a pillow.

"Yo, Colter, is everything...?" The security guard who was stationed outside pokes his head inside the locker room, takes one look at me in Colter's arms with his hands on my boobs, and snaps his mouth closed. He slowly pulls back, disappearing from the doorway.

"Shit," Colter whispers into the ensuing silence.

My cheeks blaze with humiliation. The security guard now thinks I'm a puck bunny too. He probably believes I came back here to have pity sex with Colter after he got kicked out of the game.

This is Silver Spoon Falls. Gossip travels at the speed of light around here. By next week, it'll be all over town. Razor, my brother-in-law, will find out, and then my sisters, and my brother. It'll be the Grand Inquisition. And any chance I had of settling quietly into this town will vanish in a puff of smoke. Everyone will think I landed this story by sleeping with Colter and not through my own hard work.

"Leia, wait," Colter growls, reaching for me when I jerk out of his arms, trying to put distance between us.

"Getting caught naked with a woman in a locker room may make you look good, but it doesn't make me look good, Colter. I came here to do a job. Leave me alone and let me do it!" I cry, stomping toward the doors. "And for the love of God, put on some freaking pants!"

"This isn't over!" he shouts as I rush out of the locker room with my head down.

CHAPTER TWO

Colter

"This is such bullshit," I growl to Coach Grayson Marrow, shoving my stuff into my bag. "You know Gordon started every single one of those altercations."

"I know," Coach says, clasping my shoulder. "Jordan knows it too. But you got a game misconduct. We're the new kids on the block. We have to play by the rules."

"Well, the rules are bullshit." I slam my locker before looping my bag over my shoulder. I've been playing professional hockey long enough to know there is no fighting this suspension, though. Our next game is Saturday. If I don't take the suspension on the chin, the President of the League will lengthen the suspension after his review. We can't afford that. I'd rather be out one game than three.

But fuck Bruce Gordon, for real. I don't know what his problem is, but he's a menace.

"Any idea why he was gunning for you so hard?" Coach asks, walking me toward the doors.

"Not a fucking clue." I rake a hand through my hair, still not sure what I did to piss in the man's Cheerios. Five years ago, we played on the same team. We were never close, and he's always been a douche. But we were never enemies either. Whatever crawled up his ass last night felt personal, though.

Coach lifts his chin in a nod. "Guess he had something to prove."

"Guess so," I mutter, not entirely sure what he was trying to prove. That he can take a beating? That I can still outskate him? Don't know and don't care to find out. Leia is the only good thing to come out of the entire shitshow that was last night's game. Well, her and the fact that we won.

Leia, the smart-mouthed little troublemaker who melts like sugar as soon as I touch her. Fuck, she's pretty with her blonde hair and sky-blue eyes. She looks like she belongs in a classroom, teaching kindergarten. But there's a sort of steel in her eyes that makes my dick hard. She's trouble with a capital *T*. I should know because I've caused enough of it.

I play hockey because it keeps me grounded. I need structure in my life. Hockey gives me that in spades. We wake up early and train until we're too fucking exhausted to do anything else. And then we get up and do it all over again. That's been my life since I was fourteen. Before that? Well, it was either hockey or juvie for me. I was not a good kid.

I had too much free time and a penchant for pulling pranks that weren't always legal. Hockey straightened me out. By the time I finished my first game, I was hooked. I still play the occasional prank on my teammates—we razz the shit out of one another—but they're harmless.

Is whatever Leia doing harmless? I don't know. She was dead-set against telling me what she was doing in our locker room. I don't believe for a second that she got lost, though. I reviewed the security footage. She snooped through several other rooms before she found our locker room.

Did she think it was the Stingrays' locker room?

If I can't fly out with the team tomorrow for the game on Saturday, it'll give me a chance to track down the curvy little goddess and ask her myself. She's been occupying ninety-nine percent of my brain since last night. It's driving me crazy. Actually, the possibility that she was trying to sneak into the Stingrays' locker room to meet Bruce Gordon is driving me crazy. There's no goddamn way I'm letting her anywhere near him.

She's mine. I decided that about five seconds after I met her. There's something about her that I want to lay claim to in the most primal way possible. Maybe that's fucked up, but I don't really care. I'm going to ruin her for anyone else. Just as soon as I find out who the fuck she is.

With a name like Leia, I don't figure it'll be that difficult in a town this size.

"Be here for the team meeting tomorrow!" Coach shouts after me. "Your ass isn't off the hook just because you're not flying out for the game."

"Yeah, yeah." I duck through the doors and run right into Miles Tempest. His long hair is pulled back away from his face, which is set in a dark scowl. There's a reason everyone calls him Temper. He's a cranky fucker, which makes it far too easy to mess with him.

"You!" he growls, smacking me in the chest with a book. "You did this!"

I glance at the cover of the book and double over with laughter. "Jesus Christ, Miles. I'm not one to judge a kink, but tentacles, man? Really?"

He growls at me again before snatching the book back from me. "I didn't buy it. You did! You had the love of my life deliver it to me." His face turns red. "I'm going to murder you, bring you back to life, and then murder you again."

"Holy shit," I whisper, clinging to the bar on the door as I laugh so hard I fucking wheeze. "They delivered it *in person*? I thought they'd just send it in the mail."

"So it was you!"

"Obviously."

"You have to go to the bookstore and tell them it's yours."

"Uh, fuck no."

"You're going." Miles smacks me in the chest with the book again like it's a goddamn weapon.

"Uh, no, I'm not." Hell to the no, I'm not walking my big ass in the bookstore and telling them I bought it for me. He's lost his mind. Unlike Miles, I don't have connections here to help smooth my way. If I become Tentacle Porn Guy, I'll never live that shit down.

"You're going," he says, narrowing his eyes at me. "Or I'm telling Razor Montgomery what Alec saw in the locker room last night."

I open my mouth and then close it, the satisfaction in his eyes making me wary. He knows something I don't. Razor Montgomery used to play guitar for *Bent*, one of the biggest rock bands in the world, before they retired. He lives here in town and is one of our biggest supporters. He and Jordan, the owner of the Falcons, are close. But why the fuck would he care that Alec walked in on me and Leia in the locker room last night? "What does Razor Montgomery have to do with anything?"

Satisfaction turns to smug triumph as Miles smirks at me. "You don't even know who the fuck you were messing around with last night, do you?"

"It wasn't like that."

"Leia Marsh is Razor's sister-in-law."

Fuck me. Razor Montgomery is going to kill me if he finds out I was feeling up his sister-in-law in our locker room last night with my cock out. He's going to be especially pissed if he finds out someone walked in and is spreading that shit around. The last thing I need right now is one of our biggest supporters riding the hate train because our security guard is running his damn mouth about my business. He has the power and influence to have me booted at the end of the season.

Funny how that should be my primary concern, but ninety percent of my brain is focused on the fact that I now know Leia's full name. I can figure out what she was really doing here last night, make her fall for me, and keep Razor from wanting to kill me. It's a win-win-win. And if I just so happen to fuck my kid into her in the process, well, I won't be sad about that.

Right after I deal with Alec for running his mouth. That shit is about to stop immediately. Leia isn't a fucking puck bunny, and I won't have anyone talking about her like she is.

"You're coming with me to the bookstore or I'm telling Razor about your little liaison," Miles says.

And there's the wrench in my plans. A pissed-off, six-foot-sized wrench.

"It's just a book, Miles," I growl.

"My fucking soulmate delivered it to my doorstep, you dick." He smacks me across the chest with the offending book again. "She thinks I have a tentacle fetish. You're fixing it. *Today.*"

I take pity on him. If I fucked up his one shot with this woman, I'll feel bad for the rest of my life. And he'll never forgive me. I'd rather be humiliated than have that on my conscience. I may like jokes, but I prefer the harmless kind. This one kind of blew up in my face.

"Fine," I sigh. I guess I'm dealing with this shit first and then dealing with Alec. "I did the crime; I'll do the time. But if you breathe a word about last night, I'm telling your girl everything I know about you. Including about that time you had food poisoning."

His face pales. "You wouldn't."

If it were just my reputation at stake, he's right, I wouldn't. But Leia is the one at risk of being labeled a puck bunny here, not me. She was upset enough last night, and she did nothing wrong. That was all on me. I'm the one who wouldn't put pants on when she asked. I'm the one who couldn't keep my hands to myself. And I'm the one who will move heaven and earth to make sure she doesn't suffer because of it.

"I wouldn't even hesitate," I growl, grabbing the book from Miles. "Let's get this humiliating shitshow on the road. I've got a situation of my own to handle."

CHAPTER THREE

Leia

"Crap." I grab Elysa's arm, dragging her into the cramped breakroom as a familiar set of broad shoulders steps out of Daniel Clifford's office. The stench of burnt coffee and old banana peels clogs my nose as my heart slams against my ribcage. A curious mix of excitement and existential dread rushes through me. "What is *he* doing here?"

Surely hockey players have more important things to do than harass reporters?

"Who?" Elysa shuffles me to the side to peer out of the narrow doorway. "Oh. *Hello*, daddy."

"Shh!" I haul her back into the room by her belt loops. "Don't let him see you."

"Okay, okay. Jeez, girl." She blinks inquisitive eyes at me before blowing strands of raven hair out of her face. "Care to tell me who he is and why we're hiding from him?"

"We aren't hiding. We're taking a break." We never take breaks in here, for obvious reasons. It's tiny, it stinks like Lawson's bananas, and there are no windows. It's just a wooden table, a fridge, and two benches. We prefer sunlight.

"Okay, then I'll just go out there and say hello." Elysa turns like she's going to make good on her threat. The flirty hem of her shirt flows around her as she spins.

Oh, she's good.

"Fine. We're hiding!" I squeak, grabbing her before she steps into the hallway and reveals my hiding place to the big jerk. I don't want to see him right now. Or maybe I do. Either way, I am so not going out there.

"I knew it! Who is he? Why are we hiding?" Her excited gaze flits across my face. "Is he the reason you've been acting weird all day?"

"I have not been acting weird." It's a total lie. I've been off my game all day. I didn't even hear Daniel calling my name at the staff meeting this morning. Copyediting sent my piece on *Mina's Place,* the new women's shelter opened by Autumn and Zane Montoya, back twice. And don't even get me started on the nine thousand times I've thought about the big jerk currently standing outside Daniel's office.

He did something to me last night, worked some sort of magic on me or cursed me. I don't know. But I can't keep him off my mind. I tossed and turned all night, thinking about his hard body pressed to mine.

It's infuriating. Truly. He's the last person I should be thinking about, considering what he thinks about me. The arrogant, bossy, ridiculously hot, grumpy jerk.

"Spill, Leia."

She's more tenacious than my five sisters combined.

"His name is Colter Bayliss. He plays for the Falcons. I met him last night when I snuck into their locker room. He was naked. And a jerk. It was a whole thing. The end," I relay as quickly and succinctly as possible.

Elysa's eyes nearly fall out of her head. "He was naked?"

"Can we please focus on what's important here?" I groan.

"Um...I don't know why that isn't your most important detail. Have you *seen* him?"

I shoot her a dirty scowl. "Did you miss the part where I said he was a jerk?"

"No, but I also heard the part where you said he was naked."

"I hate you."

"No, you don't. You hate that I'm right."

She's right. He's freaking hot...and even hotter naked, dang it.

"Why is he here?" Her brows furrow. "Oh my gosh. Is he trying to get you fired because you snuck into the locker room and saw him naked?"

"What? No, of course not. He's here because he's a crazy person. Obviously." I'm not sure why I think she's going to buy that non-explanation. She really is worse than my sisters when it comes to ferreting out the truth. Maybe she should be the one tailing Gavin while I answer the phones around here.

"Leia Marsh," she gasps. "Is he here looking for you because you snuck out on him?"

"No." His shouted promise that this isn't over echoes through my head. I'm guessing that's why he's here.

She crosses her arms, hitting me with a patented Elysa look that screams she doesn't believe a word I'm saying.

"I didn't sneak. I stormed out after he basically accused me of being a puck bunny," I sniff. "Like I said, he's a jerk."

"Oh." Her lips twitch. "You like him."

"I can't stand him."

"Mmhmm. Then why are we hiding in the breakroom?"

"I'm avoiding another prickly interaction with the grouch," I finally say. Oh, I'm a genius! I smile, pleased with myself for thinking that one up. For a minute there, I wasn't sure I had a reasonable explanation that didn't involve confessing to the rest of the humiliating night. I love Elysa, but I'm not ready to discuss the fact that Colter had his hands on my body. I do not want to dissect why I liked it. And I am taking the part about the security guard to my grave.

Elysa peeks her head out the door and then jumps back a step. "Um, you know how you said you're avoiding him? I think you should have chosen a room with another exit."

"What? Why?" I poke my head out into the hall...and come face to face with Colter's broad chest. I gulp, jumping back a step. Crap. I'm busted.

"Ah, there she is," Daniel says, smiling pleasantly.

"Indeed," Colter murmurs, his hazel eyes running up and down my body.

I try to scowl at him, but I'm pretty sure I just shiver and whimper instead. He looks far too delicious in his faded black t-shirt and blue jeans. Both fit him perfectly. I can see the way his muscles move every time he breathes. It's really unfair that God has favorites. Heaven needs a complaint department.

"Colter explained that he's helping you with your story," Daniel says, beaming at me. "Smart thinking, getting someone on the inside to help you look into whether there's illegal betting going on."

Colter's eyebrows fly upward.

Crap. Now he knows what I was doing there last night.

Before he can say anything, Elysa pops out into the hallway beside me. She throws a bright smile Colter's way before thrusting a hand in his direction. "It's nice to meet you. I'm Elysa," she says. "Leia's best friend. She was just telling me about you."

"Oh, really?" He glances from her to me, a smirk dancing at his lips. "Good things, I presume."

"Nope." Elysa smiles brighter. "But that's going to change by the end of the day, isn't it, Colter?"

I bite my lip, fighting laughter as his smirk slips. I love Elysa. She's ride or die, no matter what. I'm so glad she's the first friend I met in Silver Spoon Falls.

"Yes?" Colter says, sounding unsure.

"Of course it is." She pats him on the chest and then releases his hand to loop her arm through Daniel's. "We should let them get to work."

"Well, I..." Daniel huffs, frowning like he's not entirely sure he's on board with this plan. But Daniel is Daniel, and Elysa is Elysa. She's nothing if not determined.

She leads our boss away, chattering about needing his help with the fax machine.

As soon as they're out of earshot, I whip around to face Colter again. I think about letting him have it right here in the hallway but grab his shirt instead and drag him down the hall.

"Damn, Trouble. You that excited to get me alone?" he asks, amusement in his voice.

"Only so I can kill you," I growl, dragging him into my office. As soon as the door closes behind us, I whirl to face him. "You told my boss that you're helping me with my story? Are you insane?"

He leans back against the door, smirking. "Missed you too, goddess. How'd you sleep last night? I slept like shit, thanks for asking."

"You...I...you..." I trail off with a muffled growl, which he seems to think is hilarious. His smirk only grows. "You are such a freaking pain in my—"

He moves like lightning striking. One minute, he's leaning against the door. The next, I'm pressed against the wall with his knee wedged between mine and his lips inches from mine. The gold flecks in his eyes threaten to drag me under his spell. Or maybe that's his scent. Or the feel of his body pressed against mine. Or the warmth rushing through me in waves. Or all of it. I don't know. But good grief, it hurts in places it shouldn't.

"That's not pain, Trouble," he murmurs. "That's desire."

For a minute, I think he read my mind, and then I realize he's talking about what I was saying before he interrupted.

"You feel me right here." He grinds his knee against my center.

A blast of pleasure rips through me. I jolt upward, shocked. "Colter!"

"Told you, goddess." His mouth touches mine. "So how about you stop pretending you don't feel anything when we both know I light you up like a livewire?"

"In your dreams," I lie.

He bites my bottom lip. "No, in my dreams, you're on your hands and knees with that ass in the air."

I guess his weren't so different from mine then. Not that I'm telling him that. "How unoriginal," I mutter, feinting boredom even though my entire system threatens to overheat at any moment. "I slept like a baby. Didn't dream at all."

"Liar. I bet I rode you hard in your dreams, didn't I? Did I leave an ache between your thighs, pretty baby?" He licks into my mouth, kissing me as if he's trying to steal my soul. I melt beneath him, melt *for* him. My God, this man can kiss. "Did you hate waking up without me?" He teases my tongue into an erotic dance before backing off. "I fucking hated waking up without you, Leia."

I'm all twisted around him like a blanket, clinging to him. My mind commands my body to let him go, but my body refuses to cooperate. It's firmly on board with whatever sexual voodoo he's working on me. I think my heart may even be working in his favor.

My head, though? Well, it's a little slower to forgive.

"You were at the arena last night for your story," he says after a moment, perhaps realizing I'm not ready to have the conversation he's pushing for. Not yet.

"I told you that's why I was there."

"Thought you were trying to meet Gordon," he mutters.

And there it is. The reason my head is not on board with the rest of me. A scowl overtakes my expression. I drop my hands from around his neck and push against his chest, trying to force him back a step. "Back up, Colter," I demand, my voice shaking.

He steps back, eyeing me like he thinks I might bite.

"I'm not a puck bunny," I growl.

"I never said you were."

"This is the second time you've accused me of being there to hook up with a player." I cross my arms, glaring at him. "Contrary to popular opinion, not every woman on the planet wants to sleep with every hockey player she comes across."

"I wasn't accusing," he says, his voice soft.

I snort.

"I was conjuring up worst-case scenarios because I was jealous as hell, Leia." Those hazel eyes burn me with sincerity. "Contrary to popular belief, not every hockey player sleeps with every woman he comes across." He flashes that smirk at me again. "I don't fuck around either, but that mouth has been driving me crazy since you broke into the locker room last night."

I roll my eyes, softening incrementally. He means it. I'm not sure how I know he does, I just know. He doesn't think I'm a puck bunny. He isn't trying to sleep with me because he thinks that's what I do. And I don't think this is something he does regularly, either.

"I didn't break into the locker room. I had a press pass."

"You were looking for the Stingrays' locker room," he growls, eyes narrowed. "Why? What do they have to do with illegal betting?"

"Maybe nothing. Maybe something. I don't know yet."

"Care to explain?"

"Care to explain why you told my boss you were working on this story with me?" I ask instead of answering.

"Because I am working on it with you." He holds his arms out. "You need an inside man. You got it, Trouble."

"Nope. No way."

He lets his arms fall. "Why the fuck not?"

"I'm trying to fly under the radar, Colter. Having a giant hockey player tagging along is the exact opposite of flying under the radar."

"You think there's illegal betting going on at the arena, right?"

"Something like that," I mutter, eyeing him sideways. And then I huff. "Why would hockey players from other teams meet with a bookie here?"

"Who the fuck was meeting with a bookie?"

"I'm not sure I should say."

"Gordon," he guesses, reading my expression.

"Maybe." I chew on my bottom lip. "Your team has played two games here. I've seen players from both teams meeting with the same bookie before the games. Why would they do that?"

"Gambling addictions? Illegal betting? Match throwing? Could be any number of reasons they'd meet with a bookie." Colter scowls, pacing around my office. It's cramped to begin with thanks to the eight filing cabinets Daniel insists on keeping in here, but it feels even smaller with Colter in here. "You're sure they were meeting with a bookie?"

"They met in an alley behind the arena. I got photos of them exchanging money. And the bookie is Elysa's situationship, Gavin. They were definitely meeting a bookie."

"Situationship?" A ghost of a smile touches Colter's lips.

"She's avoiding him because he's a bookie but hasn't broken up with him. It's a whole complicated thing." I wave away the question. "It doesn't even matter."

"Fuck, you're cute when you ramble."

"Colter!"

He blinks and then rapidly shakes his head like he's trying to clear cobwebs from his brain. Or, knowing what I know about him, it's more like he's trying to clear dirty thoughts from it. "Sorry, Trouble. You start rambling, and I hear the goddamn angels sing."

He's shameless. Truly.

"Oh my God. Please, leave my office." *Before I fall in love with you, and you break my heart.*

"What about our story?"

"My story, Bossy. It's *my story*." I step behind him, plant my hands in the center of his back—an hello, muscles—and gently push him across my office.

He balks at the door, spinning around to grab me at the last minute. My plan to kick him out goes up in smoke as his mouth slants down on mine.

"You love kissing me." He breaks away from my mouth to gloat.

"Shut up, Colter." I drag his mouth back down to mine like the greedy, crazy woman he's turned me into.

We end up making out for five full minutes before he pulls back with a groan. His wild hazel eyes meet mine. "That goddamn mouth is dangerous, Trouble." He swipes a thumb along my bottom lip, shaking his head. "You better finish kicking me out before I do something you regret, or we get caught again."

My stomach twists itself into knots at the reminder of what happened last night. We can't do that again. Gossip runs rampant in small towns, especially ones like Silver Spoon Falls. I don't want to be the next victim for the mill when I just moved here. Charlie and Adalynn have already been fodder. The whole town probably thinks our family is crazy. It's my job to protect us. It's what I've always done. Protect my sisters.

I slip out of Colter's arms and instantly wish I was back in them.

I am so confused. I desperately need to talk to Adalynn and Heidi. Maybe they can help me sort out why Colter gives me butterflies and scares me simultaneously.

"Go home, Colter," I whisper.

"I'm not giving up," he warns me, leaning down to press his lips to my forehead. "I'm going to keep chasing until you're ready to quit running, and then I'm making you mine, Leia."

He straightens and strides from my office, closing the door behind him.

CHAPTER FOUR

Colter

"H ey."

I glance up as Noah Diamante drops down onto the bench beside me, his dark hair still damp from the shower. "What's up?"

"You good, brother?" he asks, his obsidian eyes serious as he holds a fist out for me to bump.

"Yeah, fine."

His brows slash together, his expression making it clear he thinks I'm bullshitting him as I bump his fist. I was pissed after the game and he knows it. Not that anyone could blame me. I got booted from the game, and then I ran Leia off with my mouth. It wasn't a great night.

I felt like a dick for making her feel like a puck bunny. Actually, I *was* a dick for making her feel that way. She's a goddess, no doubts about it. But she's safe with me. One way or another, I'm going to convince her of that too.

"You sure?"

"Positive," I grumble, shaking my head. Noah would be in the NHL if he hadn't fucked up his knee his rookie year. It still gives him problems occasionally. Any dreams he had of playing in the majors went up in smoke. But he's settled into the AHL like it's his home. He looks out for everyone, takes care of everyone, and makes sure we all have our heads on straight. He's good people.

He jerks his chin in a nod, and then gives me a sly smirk. "Good because these fuckers are about to razz the shit out of you and I don't want you going for their throats," he mutters with a laugh. "You earned every minute of it."

"What the fuck did I do?"

He opens his mouth to answer but doesn't get a chance.

"Tentacles!" Atlas Jacks, our oversized goalie, booms, waltzing into the locker room. His green eyes light up as he rubs his hands together and then points at me. "I fucking knew you were a freaky bastard, Bayliss."

"Miles, you son of a bitch," I growl.

"That's what you did," Noah says ruefully.

I climb to my feet to grab my phone out of my locker. I'm sending a giant bag of dicks to Miles' house. The glitter bomb kind that explodes when it's opened so he's seeing glitter dicks for the rest of his life.

"I don't have a fucking tentacle kink. Miles blackmailed me." I open the locker, only for a giant damn octopus to come flying out at my face. "What the fuck?"

I leap backward, startled. The stuffed octopus falls to the floor at my feet.

Atlas howls with laughter, clinging to Jensen Sparks to keep himself upright. Even Noah laughs his ass off.

"I hate all of you," I mutter in disgust, snatching the octopus up and stuffing him back into the locker. I'm going to find Miles and kill him. Painfully.

Two hours later, I call Reid Lawless from the parking lot of Leia's office where I'm camped out. I agreed to give her space yesterday, but I never said how much space I was giving her. Especially not now that I know what story she's chasing. Bookies can be dangerous, even in a town like this.

I convinced Coach to let me out of practice after the team meeting so I could follow her today. He wasn't thrilled, but since I'm suspended anyway, it's not like missing one day on the ice is going to hurt anything. I'll make it up to him next time. He knows I will.

I would have been useless on the ice, anyway. I couldn't keep my girl off my mind long enough to focus on the meeting. She's driving me crazy and doesn't even know it. I've never pursued a woman before. I don't even know where to start with this one. But one way or another, I'm going to break down her walls and make her mine.

I keep my eyes on the doors in case she tries to leave. I fully intend to tail her if she does. There's no damn way I'm letting her chase after a bookie by herself. She may think she's a little badass, but criminals don't much care how feisty you are when you get in their way.

"If you're calling because you want to fly to Arizona and kick Gordon's ass for getting you suspended, I'm probably in," Reid says as soon as he picks up the phone.

"Probably?" I smile, shaking my head. Reid, like me, can be a handful. Trouble just follows him naturally.

"Depends on what my wife wore to work this morning," he says. "She snuck out before I was awake. I may have to take a raincheck on punching Bruce Gordon in the face to spank her gorgeous ass."

"Too much information, man," I mutter. The less I know about his sex life, the better. "Way too much information. Especially since I'm actually calling for your wife."

"What the fuck, Bayliss?" Reid growls. "Why the fuck are you calling for my wife?"

"Settle down. Jesus. I didn't say I wanted to sleep with her. She's a lawyer. She knows law enforcement around here. Hell, you do too, considering they arrested your ass your first week here," I remind him. He got into a bar fight. "I need some info on someone."

"My charges were dropped, fucker. And she'd kick your ass if you even tried to hit on her. Then I'd have to kick your ass." He's a territorial bastard. We've been giving him nine kinds of hell about it, but I'm starting to get it. Just the thought of Leia meeting one of our teammates the other night had me ready to start throwing punches. "Who do you need info on?

"All I have is a first name, but he's a bookie in town."

Reid falls quiet for a moment. "What the fuck are you tangled up in, Colter?"

"I'm helping out a friend with something. Her girlfriend is dating this douche." None of that is a lie, strictly speaking. Whether Leia wants my help or not, she's getting it. And we are friends. We're going to be two peas in a damn pod real soon.

"I'll ask Wren to have Dillon call you."

"Thanks, brother."

"Don't mention it."

I disconnect and drop my phone in the console with a relieved exhale. Hopefully, the sheriff knows something about this bookie and can clue me in on what we're dealing with here. It'd be nice to know what the fuck kind of trouble Leia is chasing.

Someone taps on my window.

My heart hits my shoes. My head hits the ceiling.

"Son of a bitch," I growl, rubbing the top of my head. I peer out of the window and barely see the top of Leia's head. How the fuck did she manage to sneak out of the building on me? Jesus. She's a fucking ninja.

She cranes her head back. Her smirk lets me know she's pleased she managed to startle me. "You know stalking is illegal in all fifty states, right?"

"I'm not stalking you. I was handling business." Oh, excellent response. I barely contain a smug grin.

"Public indecency is illegal in all fifty states too," she says levelly.

Well, there goes that moment of triumph. She's impressively quick with the comebacks. It's sexy as hell. Most people go out of their way to compliment me. Not Leia. She doesn't even hesitate to mouth off and give me shit. I fucking love it.

"Did you come to see the show then, Trouble?" I ask. "Just couldn't stop thinking about me fucking my own hand, could you?"

"No. I mean no, I was not thinking about that," she squeals. "I was just leaving!"

"Liar. You've already told on yourself now."

"Have not," she mumbles, a blush climbing up her cheeks. Christ, she's so goddamn pretty with her hair pinned back from her face with a little rose pin. Her vintage black suit accentuates her full figure in all the right places, highlighting her curves. She's effortlessly stylish, and feminine, but I don't think she has a clue how damn sexy she is. Or how hard I am right now.

"Where are you going?"

"Nowhere."

"Leia."

Fire flashes in her eyes. "It's my story, Colter."

"And you won't get to write it if you end up dead in a ditch somewhere." I climb out of the truck, holding the door open for her. "Get in the truck."

She plants a hand on her hip, scowling up at me. "Has anyone ever told you that you're bossy?"

"Yeah, you. Get your sexy ass in the truck, or I can put you in the truck, Trouble. Your choice."

"Fine." She stomps forward, smacking me with her laptop bag as she passes me.

I growl, dragging her body up against mine. My mouth lands against her ear. "You trying to get us arrested for public indecency? Because the more you fuck with me, the harder you make me, Leia."

"The bag slipped," she says, her voice saccharine.

I nip her ear, groaning, "Get in the truck."

She elbows me as she clambers up into the driver's seat, muttering to herself about my big stupid truck. I chuckle, staring at her ass until she glances over her shoulder and catches me. "Stop staring at me. It's rude."

"Stop looking so fucking sexy. It's criminal."

She huffs and drops down into the passenger seat, fluffing her hair.

I climb in after her.

"Are you always like this?"

"Seatbelt, goddess." I reach across her and grab the belt before she can, carefully locking her into place. She gives me a dirty glare but doesn't try to stop me. Whether she wants to admit it or not, she loves having me in her space. I can tell by the way she trembles whenever I get close. "Like what?"

"Hmm?"

I chuckle, shifting away from her. As soon as I do, she shakes her head as if she's trying to clear it. "Am I always like what, Leia?"

"Shameless. Bossy. Like you, I guess." She leans forward and pushes the button on the glovebox. When it opens, she smiles to herself and then starts prowling through my shit.

"When it comes to you? Yes." I buckle up and then start the engine before turning back to her. She's flipping through the paperwork on my truck. "You having fun over there?"

"Just looking." She glances up at me, her gaze clear and guileless...and so full of shit it makes me chuckle. "You're due for an oil change soon."

I flick my gaze up to the sticker in the corner of my window. Shit. I am due soon.

"You checking to make sure there isn't a woman's name on any of the paperwork?"

"What? No." She scowls at me and then bites her bottom lip, rethinking her answer. "Maybe."

"There is no woman. There hasn't been a woman since college."

"Oh. Why not?"

I cock a brow. "Are you asking me why I'm not a man-whore?"

"No!" She shoves all of the paperwork for my truck back into the glovebox. "Just wondering why someone who looks like you and plays a professional sport is single." She shrugs. "It's a mystery."

"You like me." A smirk curves my lips.

"Do not."

"You do."

"No, I don't."

"Why are you single, then? You're the catch of the god-damn century."

She wrinkles her nose at me, rolling her eyes. "You're being ridiculous again."

"Nah, you are if you think saying that makes me ridicu-lous. Have you seen you?" I gape at her. "That body? The way you walk? The way you dress? The shit you say? The fact that you don't take shit from anyone, or care what anyone thinks? God*damn*, Trouble." I shake my head, speechless. If she doesn't know what a catch she is, I'm going to teach her.

She drops her gaze as a blush climbs up her cheeks, staining them pink. "Guess I never thought of it that way." A little smile dances at her lips. "I guess I am pretty awesome."

"Uh, fuck yeah, you are," I laugh. "Now, where are we going?"

"The bookstore."

I nearly choke on my tongue.

A bright peal of laughter rings out from her side of the truck. "You should see your face right now, Colter. Oh my gosh." She wipes her eyes, still laughing. "You look like you'd rather spend an eternity on the rack."

"Sign me up for that," I growl. "We aren't going to the fucking bookstore."

"Why not? I love the bookstore. There are so many interesting things there."

I narrow my eyes at her, suspicious at hell. "What did you hear?"

"About the bookstore?" She pleads ignorance, turning those wide, guileless eyes up at me. Except they shine with humor. "Why would I have heard anything about the bookstore, Colter?"

Oh, I am going to kill whoever told her. Was it Miles? I bet it was Miles. The entire team gave me shit through the whole damn meeting this morning because of him.

"I sent the damn book to Miles as a joke," I growl. "But he's in love with the chick who delivered it. So he made me go to the bookstore yesterday and tell them that it was mine so she doesn't think it's his."

"And you agreed to this?" Leia arches a brow at me.

"I had motivation." I shrug. "He knows your brother-in-law."

"Ah. He knows about the locker room?"

"Yes. But before you get pissed, Miles isn't going to say anything. And neither is Alec. I made sure of that." I threatened to go to his boss, Cormac, with the tape of him just letting her waltz right by while he played on his phone. He didn't have much to say after that. Cormac Carmichael doesn't fuck around when it comes to running security. He'll toss Alec out on his ass in a heartbeat if he knows Alec isn't taking the job seriously.

Leia sits quietly for a moment and then nods. "Okay."

"Okay?"

"I'm taking your word for it," she says quietly. "I think you mean it when you say you're here for the right reasons. And I'm really hoping I'm not wrong, Colter."

"Fuck," I groan, gripping the steering wheel like my life depends on it. I think it might right now. Because if this is a test, I'm about two seconds from failing it. I desperately want to drag her into my lap and show her exactly what I think about her confession, but I'm thinking if I do, I'll spook her. I've earned a chance with her, but I haven't earned her trust yet. Not entirely. "You're killing me here, goddess."

Her bright smile is another nail in my coffin. "Too bad, Bossy. We have a bookie to tail."

CHAPTER FIVE

Leia

"This douche is the most boring bookie I've ever tailed," Colter complains for the fifth time this afternoon, scowling at the grocery store across the street. Gavin went inside fifteen minutes ago with a shopping cart. "He's been running errands all damn day."

"You didn't have to come," I remind him, fighting a smile. It's easy to see why he plays hockey. He wouldn't last long at a desk job. He has too much energy and not nearly enough patience. "Also, when have you ever tailed a bookie before?"

"Mind your business, Trouble. Maybe I do this kind of shit all the time."

"Uh huh." I roll my eyes, curling my leg up in the seat beneath me. "And I play professional hockey in my spare time because it's fun."

He cracks a smile, chuckling. "Smart ass."

I grin at him, although he's right. Tailing Gavin is boring. He hasn't done anything interesting all day. Maybe because the next game isn't even in town? I don't know. But I'm never going to figure out what he's up to this way. "Okay, since you're helping me with this story, you can answer my questions. What do you know about sports betting?"

"Enough not to do it," Colter says. "I like my job. I'd prefer to keep it."

"You'd get fired if you bet on a game?" I root around in my bag for a pen and paper to take some notes.

"For betting on AHL games? Possibly. For betting on your own games? You're likely to be permanently banned from the league. It's essentially insider trading," he explains. "As a player on the team, you have access to information others don't, like tension in lines, plays, and player injuries. Using that to place bets on your own games gives you an unfair advantage."

"Oh. Guess I never thought of it that way." I scribble notes, trying to hit the highlights.

"Not to mention, every team in the AHL is associated with an NHL team. The NHL is strict about shit like this. Most of the guys in the AHL want to be called up to the NHL. Getting busted for betting on AHL games will sink those dreams fast."

"So why would someone do it?"

"Money talks. We aren't making bank playing for the AHL, Trouble. Most players make less than sixty a year. If the price is right, certain players might be willing to impact the outcome of the game to line their pockets."

"Seems like a lot to risk to me," I mutter, glancing up from my notebook. The parking lot of the grocery store is filling up with late afternoon shoppers. Most look like parents grabbing things on their way to pick up the kids from school. They're all in a hurry. Gavin's Range Rover still straddles two spots near the doors.

"Isn't that usually how it works?" Colter asks. "People bet the farm hoping for the mansion. They win a little and get hooked."

"You think that's what happened with Bruce Gordon? He tried to throw the game because he's hooked?"

"I'm not sure Gordon was trying to throw the game."

"You aren't?" That surprises me. Why is he helping me if he thinks Bruce Gordon is innocent?

Colter shakes his head, his brows furrowed. "He wasn't playing to lose out there," he murmurs. "His only goal was taking me out."

I consider that for a moment. Why would Bruce want Colter out of the game so badly? Why would Gavin? "I don't suppose you're a hockey prodigy, are you?"

"I played for the NHL for a few seasons before I got sent back down for an injury," he says. "But that was a decade ago. I'm good, but not like I used to be."

I sigh. "Well, there goes my theory, then."

His lips twitch. "I'm almost afraid to ask."

"There's a hockey bounty on your head," I say as dramatically as possible. "Fifty pounds to any player that takes you down."

He chuckles and then his laughter fades. He sits forward abruptly. "Fuck. Why didn't I think of that?"

"What?"

"The NFL."

"Huh?"

"Ten years ago, there was a scandal in the NFL with a team that was allegedly paying players to injure players on other teams. They called it Bountygate." Colter grabs his phone and pulls up an article before passing it over to me.

I quickly skim it, my brows climbing as I read what happened. Apparently, it was a huge deal that resulted in the team involved paying a massive fine, the coaching staff and general manager facing sanctions with the NFL, and players being suspended, though the player suspensions were later overturned since the entire situation was instigated by the coaching staff.

"Wow," I whisper, passing the phone back to Colter. "You think something like that is happening here?"

"Who met with Gavin last week?"

"Jimmy Brinks."

Colter shoves his phone into his pocket, his expression grim. "He tried like hell to needle Reid into a fight last week."

My stomach sinks.

"If bookies are paying players to injure or knock players out of games, perhaps they're trying to find a way to capitalize on a nationwide bounty system."

"That's not good."

"Fuck no, it's not," he growls. "Every goddamn sporting league in the nation will be at the mercy of bookies and the players in their pockets."

"I think we need to talk to Bruce Gordon."

"Or we can skip that bullshit and go straight to the source."

"What do you mean?"

He nods straight ahead.

I glance out of the window to see Gavin strolling toward his SUV with two bags of groceries in his hands. "We can't ask him. He'll deny everything."

"I didn't say we should ask him, Trouble," Colter says, his voice grim. "I'm a player. If we need confirmation that he's doing this, we don't have to go to Gordon or Brinks and hope they confess. All we have to do is get word to Gavin that I'm looking to make a little extra cash and let the chips fall where they will."

"That's a terrible idea."

"Why?"

"Because...because..."

"It's the best plan we've got, goddess," he murmurs, reaching out to touch my cheek. "You just don't like it because you don't want me getting hurt."

"That doesn't mean I like you," I lie.

"Yeah, it does."

"Fine, maybe it does," I grumble, my stomach quivering with nerves and anxiety. "But it's still a bad idea. We don't know anything about who he's involved with or how deep this runs or if he's working alone. He's not exactly poor, and I don't think he won his mansion gambling. So putting you on his radar may be putting you on the radar of very bad people."

"Then let's go find out."

"What? How?"

"Buckle up, Trouble," he says by way of answer. "We're going to see the Wizard."

"We're going to see *who*?"

Apparently, Sheriff Dillon Armstrong is the Wizard because Colter takes me to the Sheriff's Department. I guess that makes Silver Spoon Falls the *Land of Oz* in his crazy brain. The man is a menace, I swear.

He might also be right. He may be our best shot at figuring out what Gavin is doing that involves AHL players because I don't think Bruce Gordon is going to tell us even if we fly to Arizona to ask. He isn't going to incriminate himself, especially if the truth may cost him his career. I doubt Jimmy Brinks will, either. But if Colter offers himself up to Gavin, he'll be able to confirm whether or not Gavin is offering players cash to take out other players.

Being the one to break a story like that would be monumental. But this is bigger than just a story at this point. If bookies and illegal gambling rings are trying to gain a foothold in sports betting this way, it could be disastrous for players. How many will be injured, not just in the AHL, but in every major and minor sports league in the United States? The potential fallout is almost too big to consider.

Of course it'd happen here, where rich men come to grow richer. This town is overrun with millionaires and billionaires who move where the money takes them. Some of them—most of the ones I've met, actually—are amazing people. But most isn't all. Not a lot of people become obscenely wealthy because they're paragons of virtue.

The super rich like to accumulate wealth and hang onto it. That leaves them vulnerable to all kinds of misdeeds and dark plots. It wouldn't take much for a guy like Gavin to convince his rich friends to buy into this scheme if it offers a lucrative enough return. It makes a place like Silver Spoon Falls the perfect breeding ground for a scheme like this.

And I really thought life here would be boring. I guess I should have known better, considering Adalynn was almost kidnapped from the bar where she works right after she moved here. Boring doesn't seem to be in the cards for any of us Marsh girls.

"Why are we here?" I ask Colter as he helps me out of his truck.

"To see the sheriff. Figured if anyone knows anything about your bookie, he does." He tips my face up to his, his hazel eyes practically glowing as he examines my expression. "Not sure how I feel about letting you walk into a station full of cops looking like you do, though."

My lips pull down into a frown. I'm wearing my favorite suit. It makes my boobs look phenomenal. I may have picked it hoping I'd see Colter again today. "What's wrong with the way I look?"

"You're too fucking beautiful," he growls, genuinely distressed. "How do I even hope to be worthy of a goddess when the whole goddamn town will be trying to steal her away?"

Just like that, he slips into my heart, laying claim to the biggest piece of it. Crap. I'm falling for this madman. This is bad. This is so bad.

Oh, who am I trying to fool? I've been falling for him since I met the crazy man in the locker room. It's fast and intense, but it feels a little like breathing. If, you know, I was running a race while trying to breathe. My point is, falling for him is exciting and terrifying but it feels right, too.

"Colter?"

"Yeah, Trouble?"

"There is no competition," I whisper. "There's just you."

"Fuck." He presses his forehead to mine, exhaling a breath.

"Kiss me."

His lips touch mine. I think he intends it to be a short, chaste kiss, but neither of us are capable of that.

We end up making out against the side of his truck in the middle of the parking lot like horny teenagers. It's his fault. That mouth is a deadly weapon. As soon as he kisses me, I ignite like kindling. Every piece of me goes up in flames, burning for him.

"Goddamn, Trouble," he groans, pressing his face to my throat. "You're trying to get us arrested, aren't you? Saying shit like that when I'm already two seconds from bending you over and seeing just how smart that mouth is when you're begging me to let you come."

My core clenches as desire shoots through me. I want that. I want him. But two can play this game of his. "Maybe you'll be the one begging, Colter. You should probably start practicing now. I bet you'll sound adorable asking me for permission."

He nips my throat. "Keep fucking around, and we're going to find out how much you like being punished, Trouble. Think you can count smacks with my dick down your throat?"

Oh my gosh. He's filthy.

Wait. Why do I like it?

"Tease me again, and we'll find out," he growls in my ear before slowly peeling himself off me.

Naturally, he looks cool as a cucumber. Meanwhile, my dang legs are wobbly. He notices and smirks at me.

"Let's go talk to the sheriff, Trouble. I've got plans for you later."

Gulp.

Sheriff Dillon Armstrong isn't thrilled to see us. And by us, I mean me. He's in the lobby when we step inside. I think he's watching television, even though he has a pad of paper in his hands and is acting like he's taking notes about whatever the elderly man standing across from him is saying.

He glances from the TV to us. His gaze runs over Colter first. He quickly assesses him, gives him a nod, then looks at me. I think he ages ten years right in front of my eyes. Weary acceptance and a healthy dose of wariness enter his expression.

"Randall, I'll swing by tomorrow and talk to Jeff about the property line again. But this isn't a criminal matter. It's a civil dispute."

"He's trespassing!" Randall protests.

"He's mowing his yard for crying out loud," Dillon says, clearly exasperated with the old man. "If you don't want him running the mower right up against the property line, put up a fence, but it's got to be mowed one way or another. How do you expect him to do that without touching your side?"

"He could get a smaller mower," Randall sniffs. "The one he's using is just obscene."

"Right. Well, I can't force him to buy a smaller mower. Unless you want to start mowing along the property line ..."

"Me?" Randall sounds horrified by the prospect.

"Didn't think so." Dillon flips his notebook closed. "I'll swing by tomorrow to talk to Jeff and see what we can work out."

"Thanks, Sheriff." Randall seems satisfied with this and scurries out, beaming like he won the turf war.

"Jesus Christ," Dillon mutters to himself before he stomps toward us. "I'm ready to build a damn fence myself if it keeps Randall Johnson out of my damn office every week. No one warned me another Marsh sister was moving to town. Why didn't anyone warn me?"

"I wasn't aware you needed advanced notice about little ole me," I say, batting my lashes. Dillon's wife, Jules, works with Charlie's husband's twin. We tend to spend time with the same people.

He snorts. "How the hell else am I supposed to know when to plan my retirement? How long have you been here?"

"Six weeks."

"I'm six weeks overdue to retire, then."

Colter glances between us. "I take it she's not the only troublemaker in her family?"

Dillon throws his head back and laughs. "The only one? Shit, she isn't even the worst one."

"We aren't troublemakers," I protest.

"Charlie couldn't stay out of trouble if you paid her. She was just in here two days ago, causing me problems."

"Okay, so maybe she's the exception," I relent with a laugh. Charlie is kind of a menace.

Dillon smiles, shaking his head. "She isn't the exception, but I'll let you go with that. Why are you here? And does Razor know you're running around with a hockey player?"

"Razor isn't the boss of me," I sniff, rolling my eyes. "Colter's helping me with a story."

"Right." Dillon draws the word out, making it clear he thinks I'm just feeding him a line. "Do you make out in parking lots with everyone who helps you with a story?"

I gape at him. How could he possibly know that?

He points toward the TV.

"Crap," I whisper. It's a live feed showing different angles around the parking lot and inside the building. Every inch of space is covered...including the passenger side of Colter's truck.

"Your lipstick is smudged too."

I turn a dirty glare on Colter, who just shrugs.

"Don't look at me like that, Trouble. You're the one who started it," he reminds me.

"Revisionist history," I mutter, totally fine living in denial.

"You two been drinking the water around here?" Dillon asks, his gaze flickering between us.

"What else would we drink?" Colter eyes him oddly.

I just groan. I've heard the stories about the water in town. They're silly legends. I glance at Colter. Or maybe they aren't.

"Mmhmm." Dillon grins like the dang cat that ate the canary. "Thought so."

Ugh. We don't have time for this.

"We need to know what you know about Gavin Cochran," I say.

Dillon frowns. "Why?"

"I'm not sure yet," I admit. "It may be nothing. Or it could be the biggest scandal in sports history."

"Explain."

"We think he may be paying players to knock other players out of games in some sort of bounty system," I say.

"Why would he do that?"

"Imagine if you could not only bet on games but could bet that a player from X team would be injured, thrown out, or given a specific penalty, " Colter adds.

"Shit."

"Now, imagine if you could bet on which player that would be. That's a whole new revenue stream for bookies, especially if you're taking bets across every sports league."

"That's big money."

"Real big," Colter agrees.

Dillon worries his bottom lip with his teeth. "Do you have any proof?"

"Not yet, but I took photos of Gavin and Bruce Gordon exchanging money before the game on Wednesday," I say.

"And Gordon did everything he could to push me into getting myself thrown out of the game that night," Colter adds.

"I saw that."

"Seems odd that a player from Arizona would be meeting a bookie in Silver Spoon Falls right before the game he then got himself and another player ejected from, don't you think?" I ask Dillon.

"It's certainly fucking questionable," Dillon agrees, his tone grim.

"He's not the only one. Gavin also met with Jimmy Brinks when the Timberwolves were in town. And guess who tried to get Reid Lawless thrown out of the game?"

"Shit," Dillon growls. "I don't know much about Gavin. He used to work on Wall Street before he moved here. We've heard rumors that he's into gambling, but he tends to operate under the radar. If he's working with anyone, he's doing it quietly. I can look into him and see what I can shake loose, but we have nothing on him otherwise."

A dead-end. Great. My shoulders droop.

"Looks like my plan is the best plan we've got, goddess," Colter says.

I nod reluctantly. It certainly looks like it.

Chapter Six

Colter

"Where are we going?" Leia asks, leaning her head against the window to look at me. "You passed the street for my office."

"We're not going to your office. I'm taking you home with me." I hesitate for a minute. "Shit. I'm supposed to be a gentleman and give you a choice here, aren't I?"

"Do you want to give me a choice?"

"Fuck, no," I growl truthfully, my hands tight around the steering wheel as I head out of town. "I want to take you home, feed you, and then fuck you until you pass out. And if I'm lucky, when you wake up in the morning, I'll get to do it again."

"I like this plan," she whispers, her voice gritty.

I whip my head in her direction, shocked.

She smiles at me, a blush climbing up her cheeks. "Maybe this is the part where I'm supposed to pretend that

I don't want to go home with you, but it'd be a lie too, Colter. You're growing on me."

"Me or my dick."

She rolls her eyes. "I was going to say you, but now that you mention it..."

"Don't make me stop this truck, Trouble."

She laughs quietly and then sobers. "I've never done any of this before. Don't break my heart, Colter."

"Break it? I'm going to wrap it up in bubble wrap and keep it in a vault so no one else can ever get close to it. I want it all to myself," I say, not even joking a little bit. The more time I spend with her, the less I want to let anyone else close to her. I didn't fall in love with her. She knocked me on my ass and stole my damn heart right out of my chest.

It's fine, though. My heart belongs in her capable little hands. When she's anywhere near me, I feel as if it's trying to beat out of my chest to get to her like in one of those damn cartoons. Every second, I'm a livewire, my synapses firing at the speed of light.

My words soften her expression, lighting those sky-blue eyes. She grins at me, genuinely at ease as she settles back against her seat. "What are we having for dinner?"

I run through a list of options in the fridge and quickly realize I don't have much of anything to work with unless I go grocery shopping first. Since I thought I'd be in

Chicago this weekend, I've avoided going. "How do you feel about takeout, and I'll cook for you tomorrow?"

"Takeout from where?"

"First Class Pizza? The Trust Fund Café? The 5th Avenue Diner?" I ramble off suggestions.

"Pizza sounds good to me."

I use Bluetooth to call it in while she plays with her phone. I'm not sure who she's texting, but she mumbles to herself as her fingers fly across her screen, and then she laughs and types something else. She's so fucking cute. I don't think she knows how to be anything but sassy and playful. It's who she is at her core.

"What are you up to over there?" I ask after a minute, genuinely curious.

"Texting my sisters."

"Exactly how many sisters do you have?"

"Four."

"Jesus."

"We have a brother too."

"Your parents were busy," I mutter, shaking my head as I whip around an SUV going ten under. "I always wanted a bunch of siblings, but I was an only child. My parents are both surgeons. They didn't have much time for me. Honestly, I don't even know why the fuck they had me."

"My sisters and I are adopted," she says softly. "Um, we were taken away from our bio parents more than once. They left us to go grocery shopping the last time and just never came home. We were there for like a week before the neighbor found us."

"Jesus Christ," I whisper, my stomach twisting. I turn on the blinker to pull off onto the dirt road leading to my house. "That's fucked up, Leia."

"Yeah, it is." She sits in silence for a moment. "We were separated in foster care. Once Adalynn's foster parents realized she had four sisters, they demanded that we all be placed together with them." A smile enters her voice. "They adopted all five of us as soon as they could."

"Yeah?"

She nods, turning to smile at me. "Our parents are amazing."

Thank God. She deserves that. I don't know her sisters, but I know how much she loves them. I hear it in her voice, and see it written all over her face. They mean the world to her. I'm glad as hell they found a safe place to land, somewhere with people who love them the way they deserve. The shit they went through as little girls...no kid deserves that.

I understand how it shaped Leia, though. She's fierce because she had no choice. She's a survivor because she had to be. She went through something traumatic and horrific when she was just a little girl and came out with a spine forged from steel. Nothing stops her.

We bounce over potholes on the way up to the house. Leia sits forward, peering through the window in avid curiosity. I slow down a little to let her take it in. I live in an old farmhouse several miles outside of town. I've spent most of the last six months fixing the place up. It looks like a whole new house now, but I haven't done much with the inside.

"Wow," she whispers. "Your home is beautiful, Colter."

Is it too soon to hope like hell she wants it to be her house too? Because that's exactly what page I'm on right now. I can see her here, chasing our kids around in the big yard, making love on the patio, sassing me in the massive kitchen. Falling asleep in my arms in our bed. I want that so fucking badly I can taste it.

Who gives a shit if it's too soon? The only rules I've ever played by are the ones that keep me on the ice. The rest never mattered much to me. What people think, the things they say, none of that shit ever registered. Why should it now? This goddess isn't a puck bunny. She doesn't sleep around. I mean something to her. I don't think she'd be here right now if she weren't ready for the same thing. If anyone has anything to say about that, they can fuck right off.

I pull up in front of the doors and kill the engine, my hands still locked around the steering wheel. "It's not a home. Not yet."

"Oh. Why not?"

"Because you're not living in it."

"Colter." She blinks wide eyes at me, her lips parted as if she isn't sure what to say. As if she can't tell if I'm serious or just teasing her.

"Just thought I should lay all my cards on the table before we go inside," I say, holding her gaze. "Because this isn't a fling for me, Leia. You aren't a fling." I swallow hard. "Once I get you in my bed, I won't want you to leave it. I fully intend to play as dirty as I have to play to make you fall in love with me."

"I don't think..." She exhales a nervous breath. "I don't think you'll have to play very dirty at all, Bossy."

"Fuck," I groan, tipping my head back against the seat as my dick imprints against my zipper.

"But I am worried," she whispers.

"About what?"

"I don't want anyone to think I got this story by sleeping with you." She glances away from me, her shoulders bowed. "It may seem like a little thing to you, but it's important to me that I be taken seriously on my own merits. I don't want to start off with people thinking I only get scoops because of you."

"So we'll keep my name out of it," I say with a shrug. "I'm not here for credit, Leia. I'm here for you. You're chasing a bookie. I don't want you doing it alone. It's that simple. No one has to know I'm involved at all if you don't want them to know. How much you say is up to you."

"That doesn't seem particularly fair to you, though."

"Chasing stories isn't my job. It's yours. I'm here because you're here, plain and simple. And spending time with you is, by far, the best reward I've ever gotten in my life."

Her gaze flits across my face. "You mean that, don't you?"

"Uh, fuck yeah. You consume every thought in my brain, Trouble. I've had more fun with you than I've ever had on the ice."

Her smile chases the worry from her eyes. "You're not so bad yourself, Bossy. Your driving sucks, and you have no patience, but seven out of ten would spy with you again."

"Seven out of ten?" I growl, digging my fingers into the sides of her suit jacket to topple her against my chest. "Seven out of ten?"

She laughs loudly, trying to fight me off as I wrap my arms around her, claiming her lips in a deep kiss. As soon as I kiss her, she stops fighting and starts pulling me closer like the greedy little thing she is. Her moan goes straight to my cock. Fuck, everything about her in my arms goes straight to my cock.

She feels like silk and tastes like tart cherries.

I pull the clip from her hair, sending the long blonde tresses tumbling. Her floral scent swirls around us. "Goddamn," I groan against her mouth. "You smell delicious, pretty baby."

"So do you," she whispers, running her hands up and down my chest.

"Lean back. I want to see something." I place my hands on her hips to hold her steady as she leans back against the steering wheel. There isn't much room to work with in the truck, but I don't need much right now. I just need to see her, touch her. Christ, I can't wait.

I help strip her jacket away, leaving her in a lacy camisole that barely covers anything. It's sheer and sexy as hell. Her hard little nipples poke through it, making my mouth water.

"Colter!" she gasps, her hands flying to my hair when I wrap my lips around one.

"Shouldn't have them out if you don't want me playing with them, Trouble," I mutter before biting the right nipple.

She gasps again, rocking against my knees. Oh, she's responsive.

I slide my hand down her stomach, groaning. She's thick and curvy everywhere. I love it. There's enough of her to grab onto, enough of her to sink into. I want to glut myself on every inch of her. Fuck. Maybe that's what I'll do. Lock her in the bedroom and just keep her there permanently. Who needs hockey when I have a goddess to feast on?

"Colter," she whispers, her voice shaking as I undo the button on her pants. "W-what...?"

"I'm going to make you come, Trouble. Right here. Right now."

"We're outside," she says as if I'm unaware we're sitting in my truck. I can tell by the look in her eyes that the thought excites her though. She's adventurous, curious. As much as she wants to deny it, I think she likes to live on the edge with the threat of being caught hanging over her head.

"Mmhmm." I tug her zipper down. "And you're going to be a good girl and come all over me anyway."

She bites her lip and then moans, which is answer enough. She wants it. Aches for it. Fuck, this woman was made for me.

I keep my eyes on her face as I slip my hand into her panties, watching her expression. Her eyes widen, her teeth sinking into her bottom lip. "Fucking hell," I groan, stroking my thumb along her slit. "You're soaked, pretty baby."

"I know." She rocks her hips against my hand, panting. "Do you have any idea how uncomfortable it was to walk into the Sheriff's Department like this?"

"Poor baby," I croon. "You've been like this that long, huh?"

"Longer," she gasps as I part her folds and home in on her clit. Christ, she's burning hot against my fingers.

"All day?"

"Longer."

"Fuck." I grind my thumb against her clit, watching as her eyes roll back in her head. Her lips part on a whimper as she rocks her hips against my hand again, eager for more. I give it to her, all my attention focused on her and how damn beautiful she is in this moment. Jesus, I've never seen a more perfect sight than her. "How long, Leia?"

"Days," she moans. "Since I met you."

Fuck me. She's wanted me just as badly as I've wanted her the past few days. I knew it, but hearing her confirm it is something else. If she doesn't fall for me, it's going to destroy me. There's no way I'll survive losing her now. She's already embedded so deeply under my skin nothing will ever get her out again. She's a permanent part of me now, as vital to me as air or water.

"Ride my hand, Leia. Let me see how fucking beautiful you are when you're coming on me," I growl, working her juicy cunt like it's my mission. "Let me hear you, pretty baby."

"Colter. Oh my god."

She circles her hips, grinding against my hand.

For several long moments, the only sounds are my fingers sliding through her wet folds and her moans. And then I register the sound of tires moving over the gravel behind us. Fuck. The pizza guy is here...and Leia is right on the edge. Her pussy flutters around my fingers.

She hears the car a few seconds after I do. Her eyes fly open on a gasp.

"Don't stop," I growl. She's fully clothed and the windows are tinted dark enough to keep him from seeing anything more than the shapes of us. At worst, he'll see her sitting on my lap, but she doesn't know that. "Not until you come."

"Colter." She drops her gaze to mine.

"Don't. Stop."

She nods, excitement firing in her eyes. Her cunt clenches around my finger. She couldn't deny how much the thought of getting caught excites her if she wanted to, not when I can feel her body responding to it. Her honey practically drips down my wrist, she's so wet now.

I curl my fingers up, stroking her G-spot. She rocks her hips, her gaze dancing from me to the car behind us and then back to me.

"Think he'll hear you screaming when you come, Leia?" I ask, running my thumb in slow circles around her clit. "Think he'll peek in the windows to get a better look at you riding my hand like a good little girl?"

"Colter," she moans.

His car door slams.

"He's coming this way, pretty baby. Any minute now, he's going to spot us in the truck and see what I'm doing to do you. He will know I've got my hands down your pants, and you fucking love it." I wrap my hand around her throat, pulling her down to me. "He's going to know you *wanted* to get caught."

She cries out, her body locking up as that sends her over the edge. She falls forward, collapsing against my chest as the orgasm rips her apart. She writhes through it, panting my name into my throat. I hold her against my chest, my face buried in her hair, one hand still in her panties.

Jesus. I love this woman. So fucking much it's slightly terrifying.

I keep one eye on the pizza guy as he passes by the truck. He doesn't even spare us a glance. I don't think he has a clue we're in the truck. He's got his head down, looking at something on his phone.

Once he leaves, I carry Leia inside. I intend to run back out and get the pizza, but she locks her legs around me as soon as we're over the threshold, and every damn plan I had to feed her before I fuck her flies right out of the window.

I pin her to the door and take her mouth in a hot kiss.

"I want you," she whispers against my lips, pulling at my t-shirt.

I lean back long enough to rip it off over my head.

She reaches for me like a kid in the candy store.

"Nu-uh." I grab her hands, shaking my head. "Your turn. Lose the top, Trouble."

She huffs at me and then quickly yanks her camisole off before tossing it down, leaving her in a simple black bra. "Happy now?"

"Nope. Bra too."

"Bossy," she mumbles, leaning away from the door to unhook it. It falls forward before she quickly strips it off.

Her tits are perfect.

"Damn," I breathe, leaning forward to pull her left nipple into my mouth.

Her head hits the door with a faint thud. She drags her nails down my shoulder blades, moaning. I could die happy hearing that sound. Who am I kidding? This right here is my paradise.

I lave the flat of my tongue across her nipple and then blow on it.

She moans louder. And then louder when I roll the other between my fingers.

I grind my hips against her, my dick so fucking hard it hurts. Jesus. I need inside her like yesterday. This is torture. I've never wanted anything the way I want this woman bare beneath me.

I drag her away from the door and stumble into the living room with her. We land in a heap on the sofa, knocking it back several inches. Oh well. I've got more important shit to deal with than furniture scuffs on the floor.

"Lift up," I demand, slipping to my knees beside the couch.

She lifts her hips, letting me yank her pants and panties down her legs. I leave her fuck me heels on—those can stay—and then drape her legs over my shoulders.

"What are you doing?" She eyes me warily.

"I'm about to eat you for dinner, so behave and don't interrupt."

She whimpers, squirming on the couch beneath me.

I run my lips up the side of her leg, groaning. "I can already smell how sweet you are, Leia. I was right all along. You are trouble." I nip her inner thigh. "Big trouble."

"Yeah? I think you like trouble, Colter," she whispers.

"Like it?" I flick my gaze up to her. "I fucking love it."

Her eyes go wide with shock.

I don't give her a chance to respond. I bury my face in her cunt like the starving, desperate man she's turned me into. I've been thinking about this for two damn days, dreaming about making her come on my tongue. I can't wait another second.

"Colter!" Her hips lift off the sofa as she shouts my name.

I hook an arm over her waist, dragging her back down beneath me as her honey flows across my tongue like wine. She tastes as sweet as she smells. Goddamn. She's addictive. I spread her wider, growling when I feel her heels digging into my back.

"You didn't warn me you tasted like my new addiction, Leia. Now, we're both in trouble."

"I didn't know!" she cries. "I didn't...I didn't... Oh my god, Colter. What are you doing to me?"

"Making sure you forget other men exist," I growl, thrusting my tongue into her hole. I eat her out, being loud and messy. The filthy sounds spur me out. I spread her cheeks so I can get deeper, eat more of her. "Getting you addicted too."

"Yes," she moans, lifting her hips to rock against my face. "It feels so good. So damn good."

I pull her clit into my mouth, sucking hard.

She practically levitates as she explodes apart without warning, her mouth open in a silent cry. Her sticky honey floods my mouth, dripping down my chest. I groan, burying myself face first in her pussy like it's the damn holy grail. I don't need to breathe. Who needs air?

I lick and suck and feast until I can't take it anymore. My dick is going to break off if I don't get inside her now.

I place a kiss on her clit and slowly place her legs back on the couch. She sucks in one deep lungful of air after another, her body limp and sated. She's wrecked and more perfect than ever.

"You're beautiful," I murmur, rising to my feet long enough to strip out of my pants and shoes. I kick them away before lifting her into my arms. I settle back on the couch, locking her legs around my waist.

She wraps her arms around my waist, moaning when my dick grinds against her clit. This may not be the ideal position for her first time. I don't know. But I want her in my arms, face to face. I want to hold her while I make love to her.

"Are you ready to be mine, Leia?" I brush her hair away from her face to run my lips across her sweaty skin.

"Yes," she whispers, her eyes fluttering open. Those sky-blue eyes meet mine, full of confidence. "I'm ready, Colter."

Yeah, she is. Fuck.

I brush my lips against hers, coaxing her into a soft kiss as I lift her up. She tenses slightly. "I'll be gentle since it's your first time," I promise. "I don't want to hurt you."

"I don't think you're capable of hurting me."

She's right about that. I'd rip my own heart out before causing hers the least amount of pain. But this is different. I'm not a saint, but I've never done this before, either. Never been in love. Never slept with someone who owns me. This is brand new to me, and I want to get it right. She *deserves* for me to get it right and not be one of those assholes who make the first time a painful memory.

"Kiss me, pretty baby," I breathe, pressing my forehead to hers.

She offers her lips up to me willingly. I lay claim to her mouth, trying to kiss my way into the very fabric of her being. I can't get enough of her or how she responds to me. She's so eager, so explosive. When I touch her, it's like fucking fireworks every time.

I slowly sink her down onto me, taking my sweet time. It's the most painful pleasure, the most heavenly torture. She's burning hot around me and so fucking tight. There's no way I'm going to last long. I ache to slam her down on me and pound into her until we're both too sated to move. But I don't do that. I take my time and make her take hers, inch by excruciating inch.

She tenses as I tear her virgin barrier. A soft gasp whispers from her lips. My stomach twists into knots. I freeze, barely daring to breathe.

"Breathe, pretty baby," I murmur, running my lips all over her face. "That's it. You're doing so fucking good."

She exhales a shaky breath, her body relaxing. "I'm okay."

"Yeah, you are." I press my face to her throat, breathing her in. "God, you're amazing. You're taking me like a goddess, Leia."

Her inner muscles clench around my cock. I growl in ecstasy...in agony. I hardly know which anymore. She's like a vise around me, and I'm slowly losing my mind here. I need to move. Desperately.

"You like the praises, huh?" I drop her another inch and then another before pressing my mouth to her ear. "Fuck, pretty baby. Just a little bit more. Can you take a little bit more for me?"

"Colter," she moans. "Yes."

"Mm. That's my good girl." I nip her shoulder, dragging her down another inch. "Do you know how good you feel wrapped around me? You're driving me crazy, Trouble."

"Same," she gasps, clawing at my shoulders. "Colter, more. Please."

"Yeah? You're ready for more already?" I slip my free hand into her hair, tipping her head back to force her to meet my gaze. "You're such a fucking good girl, taking me like you were born for me."

She sobs my name, her inner muscles, clenching around me again.

Fuck. She doesn't just like praise. She loves it. I store that away for later. I'll be using it often, especially if it makes her this hot for me. She's leaving her claw marks all up and down my back, and she's so wet, I feel her dripping onto me.

"I want to know how good you can be, Leia. Are you ready to take all of me?" I hold her still above me, letting the anticipation build.

"Yes. Do it."

"Mm, look at how eager you are. Fuck," I groan. She has no idea how sexy she is right now, stripped bare, all her walls down, begging me to fuck her. I'm not sure which of us wants it more at this point. Her? Me? We're drowning together. And fuck, what a way to go.

I yank her the rest of the way down on me, not stopping until her ass lands against my lap. She throws her head back, shouting my name into the room as her inner muscles squeeze the fuck out of my cock.

She sobs my name, squirming on top of me. I don't have to do anything. She's so lost in ecstasy she does it herself...lifts herself up and then drops back down, chasing the pleasure. I watch through slit lids, enamored of her and the look on her face.

"Fuck," I groan, gripping her hips. "Just like that, pretty baby. Keep fucking me just like that."

"Need you," she gasps.

I instantly pull her closer. "What do you need, Leia? You need more?" I lift her up and drop her harder. "You need faster?" I pick up the pace, practically bouncing her on my lap. "You need me to tell you how fucking incredible you feel? You're wrecking me, pretty baby. Christ, you take me so fucking well, I can't breathe."

"Yes!" she sobs.

I don't know which part she's saying yes to, so I give her more of everything. I go harder and faster. I whisper how good she feels and tell her how good she's doing. Words spill from my lips in a steady stream as I fuck her, driving us both toward the edge of a cliff. Her inner walls flutter and pulse around my dick, her cries of ecstasy growing louder and louder.

"That's it, pretty baby," I groan, grinding her against the root of my cock every time she lands on my lap. "You're so close now. I can feel your thighs shaking. Fuck." I press my face to her throat again, kissing and nipping at her skin. "You're going to come all over me, aren't you?"

"Y-y-yes," she whimpers. "God, yes."

"Good girl, Leia. God, you're such a good girl for me." I pump my hips and then rock her against me, using everything I have to get her there before I come. "Give it to me, pretty baby. Come for me before I lose my damn mind." I drop her down on me, grinding her clit against me again.

She embeds her nails in my shoulders, chanting my name as the dam breaks. Her cunt flutters around my cock as she comes, soaking me with her juices. I growl in ecstasy as my balls give up the fight and I fall over the edge with her.

The whole damn world goes black as cum shoots up my shaft, pouring into her. I think my heart stops beating for a minute. The only thing that exists is her. Leia, my curvy goddess with the smart mouth who waltzed into the locker room and changed my entire fucking world.

CHAPTER SEVEN

Leia

"Can I ask you a question?" I ask Colter, fidgeting with my pizza. He scooped me up a little while ago and carried me to his bedroom. After cleaning me up, he put me in bed and told me to stay there.

He returned to the room five minutes later with pizza, beer, and a bottle of wine. I guess we're celebrating sex. Go, Team!

"Depends on the question."

"It's about earlier." My cheeks heat. "Um, about what happened in the truck, I mean."

He leans back against the headboard, taking a long pull from his bottle. "What's on your mind, Trouble?"

"What does it mean?"

"What does me getting you off mean?" He smirks at me, humor dancing in his eyes.

"No." I roll my eyes at him. Why can't he ever be serious? Jeez. "The fact that I...liked...what we did? Isn't that kind of...?" I trail off with a shrug, unsure how to say what's on my mind. "I don't know. Never mind."

His smirk disappears as he sets his bottle carefully on the bedside table. "Hey," he murmurs, holding his hand out to me. "Come here."

I drop my half-eaten slice back onto my plate and scramble across the bed to him. Once I'm where he can reach me, he quickly reels me in, not stopping until I'm straddling his thighs.

"You think being turned on by the thought of getting caught makes you a hypocrite," he says.

I nod, relieved he gets it.

"You're allowed to get off on the fantasy but shy away from the reality, Trouble. They're two different things. You felt safe enough to explore the fantasy in the truck because you knew I wouldn't let anything happen to you." He rubs circles against my outer thighs. "You know I'm going to protect you."

"I did feel safe," I whisper. "But I liked thinking that he might catch us."

Colter grins, his hazel eyes darkening. "I know you did. You were sexy as hell, riding my hand like that. Maybe next time I'll fuck you somewhere you can't make noise, or dozens of people will hear you."

My core clenches at the thought.

He groans, dragging my mouth to his for a kiss. He tastes like beer, but I wrap my arms around his neck anyway, trying to intice him into more. I want a repeat of earlier.

Sex with him is mind-blowing. I'm not sure if it's supposed to be that good or if he's just that good, but holy moly. I still can't feel my toes.

"Nu-uh," he growls, breaking the kiss as he slides me off his lap. "If I get inside you again now, I won't be able to do it later, and that's unacceptable, goddess. I fully intend to fuck you to sleep tonight. You'll sleep with me inside you; that way, I can keep that greedy little pussy satisfied all night."

Oh, my goodness. He's crazy. And I love it.

"Fine," I huff, pretending to be annoyed. "But I'm hogging all the covers."

"No, you aren't. I'll be your blanket."

My phone buzzes before I can answer him. "Hold that thought," I mumble, grabbing it from the nightstand where he put it when he brought in the pizza.

Bestie: SOS!!

"Crap," I whisper, my heart jumping into my throat.

"What's wrong?"

"I need to call Elysa." I flip the phone around to show him the message.

"Call her," he orders as soon as he reads it.

I'm already dialing her number.

"I'm so sorry to interrupt whatever sex games you're playing with the hockey hunk," she blurts as soon as she answers, "But Gavin is insisting on dinner tomorrow and won't take no for an answer. I don't know what to do!"

I quickly relay the issue to Colter, who scowls. "Invite him over," he says.

"What? Why?"

"Double date, goddess."

My stomach twists itself into knots.

"It's the perfect time for me to meet him," he says quietly. "I'm suspended from Saturday's game, so he'll think I'm angry and in need of a little extra cash."

"What's he saying?" Elysa asks. "I can barely hear him."

I hesitate for a long moment before I reluctantly answer. "He wants you to invite him over for dinner with the three of us. He's going to try to get Gavin to recruit him."

"Oh," Elysa whispers. "That's pretty smart."

"It's crazy," I mutter, hating the plan just as much now as ever. I don't want to use Colter as bait, especially when we don't know nearly enough about what we're dealing with here. But I don't know what other options we have. If I don't let him do this, he's at just as much risk on the ice. Bruce Gordon already demonstrated that.

At least this way, we have a shot at stopping Gavin before he gets someone hurt or destroys someone's career.

"It's our only plan, pretty baby," he reminds me.

"I know. That doesn't mean I have to like it."

He smiles, reaching out to cup my cheek. "Believe me, Trouble, I'm not thrilled about it, either."

I sigh heavily. "Set it up, Elysa. Tell him whatever lies you have to tell him."

By the time dinner rolls around, I'm a nervous wreck. I've changed four different times and paced a hole in the floor. Elysa is in much better shape than I am, even though she's the one who has to pretend she's still into Gavin.

"I'm never dating again after this," she mutters, throwing herself down onto the couch with a dramatic sigh. "I'm going to be a crazy cat lady."

"What? No way." I twirl to face her with my hands on my hips. "You can't give up just because your first attempt didn't work out." Like me, Elysa hasn't ever dated much. She bumped into Gavin downtown one day, and he asked her out. They hadn't been dating long, but she was having fun with him. I don't want him to scare her away from trying again, especially since she was way too good for him in the first place.

She scrunches up her nose at me. "Easy for you to say. You won the dating lotto. I ended up with a dud."

I plop down beside her, resting my head against hers. "He has teammates, you know."

That perks her up. "Oh, I didn't think about that. Are they hot?"

"Probably." I shrug. "They play hockey fifty million hours a week."

"Good point."

The timer on the oven dings.

"I've got it," I say, climbing to my feet. "I need something to do anyway."

"Good, because I hate cooking." Elysa kicks her feet up on the couch with a cheeky grin.

I shake my head, laughing as I enter the kitchen to check the lasagna. The scent of tomato sauce and garlic fills the small space, making my stomach growl. I pull the oven open, and my mouth waters. It looks amazing. Elysa may not like to cook, but she's fantastic at it. Me, on the other hand? Well, not so much.

I can handle the basics, but anything beyond that is asking too much. Heidi is the sister with skills in the kitchen. Our adopted mom taught her everything she knew. She wants to open a bakery when she graduates. If anyone can do it, Heidi can.

"Damn, you look good," Colter growls behind me as I put the bread in the oven. He quickly crosses the kitchen, stepping up right behind me. His hand brushes my ass before I feel his erection grind against my ass.

"Colter," I groan, slowly rising to my feet.

He pulls me back against him, his arms wrapped around me. "Fuck, I missed you."

"You saw me this morning."

"Too long," he mutters, nuzzling my throat. "Way too fucking long."

I melt against his chest, my body heating as he kisses all over my neck. He's right. A full eight hours without seeing him is way too long. I missed him like crazy today. I kept expecting him to show up at the office. But we thought it would be best if he stayed away today, just in case Gavin decided to show up to see Elysa. Neither of us wants to give him any reason to suspect this is a setup.

"I missed you too," I whisper.

He spins me around, tilting my head back with a finger beneath my chin. "Yeah? You missed me?" His hazel eyes scan my face, his expression probing. "Enough to come home with me again tonight, goddess?"

"Maybe."

"If you don't come home with me, I'm sleeping in your bed with you. Think you can be quiet while I'm fucking you all night?"

"Colter," I groan, my blood threatening to liquefy.

"Don't *Colter* me, Trouble," he growls. "One way or another, I will be sleeping in the same bed with you tonight, and I will be fucking you until you pass out on top of me. So if you don't want Elysa to hear us, then you had better pack a bag and come home with me."

"Maybe," I say again. I'm definitely going home with him tonight. But I like teasing him. I like when he gets growly and bossy. It's kinda hot.

He narrows his eyes at me and then smirks. "You just have to fuck with me, don't you?"

"Yep, and we both know you love it."

"Yeah, I do," he says, his expression softening. "I love every goddamn thing about you, Leia."

Oh, my goodness. That's the second time he's basically told me that he loves me. He means it too. I see it lurking deep in his eyes. This crazy man is in love with me.

"Colter, I lo—"

"Gavin just pulled up," Elysa interrupts, popping her head into the kitchen.

Crap.

Colter and I reluctantly break apart, turning to face her.

"Let's get this over with," I mutter.

Elysa ducks out of the kitchen to let Gavin in. I start after her, but Colter grabs my hand, tugging me back into his arms.

"Tonight, when I'm inside you, you're going to finish what you were trying to say," he growls against my ear. "I want to hear you screaming it, Leia."

"Okay," I agree, more than willing to give him that.

He inhales a sharp breath and then releases me. "Let's get this over with."

Even though Gavin is a bookie, he's not a bad guy. Well, he doesn't *act* like a bad guy. He's always been pleasant to me. He's laid-back, always laughing and joking. It's also obvious that he really likes Elysa. He can't keep his eyes off her at dinner.

She tries her best to act like everything is fine, but she nearly chokes on her wine when Gavin brings up hockey while we're eating tiramisu after dinner.

"You okay, kitten?" Gavin asks, rubbing her back. His Rolex gleams, standing out like a sore thumb in our apartment. He probably makes more in a week than we do combined in a year. He never acts like it matters to him, but I can't help but notice the disparity today.

He's dressed in a thousand-dollar suit, his dark hair slicked back. Elysa is in a pretty black swing dress with her hair in an intricate updo. She looks gorgeous but uncomfortable. Dresses aren't really her thing. She only ever wears them for Gavin.

Does he even notice that she's uncomfortable? That she dresses up for him even though she hates it?

"Fine," she wheezes, waving him away. "Wrong pipe."

He grins at her, flashing his dimple before he turns back to Colter. "You've had a long career in the AHL," he says, his gray eyes serious. "You never wanted to move up to the NHL?"

"I started out in the NHL a decade ago." Colter sets his fork down. "Tore my ACL three seasons in and got sent down to rehab. I was out for a year before I could skate on it properly again. I knew I wouldn't get called back up my first time back on the ice."

"Damn." Gavin shakes his head. "That's a bitch."

"Yeah, it is. But I'm still playing, so it is what it is." Colter scowls. "I *should* be playing, anyway. Fucking Bruce Gordon."

"Who?" Gavin furrows his brows like he's never heard the name before. He's a good liar; I'll give him that. If I hadn't seen them meeting with my own eyes, I'd almost believe he had no clue who Bruce Gordon was.

"He plays for the Stingrays," I jump in, rolling my eyes for effect. "He couldn't play nice on the ice the other night and kept starting fights. Colter ended up suspended from the game this weekend. He's grumpy about it because the team flew out today."

"Uh, fuck yeah, I'm grumpy," Colter growls. "If I'm not on the ice, I'm not getting paid."

"You get paid by game?"

Crap. Did we just give him intel he didn't have? Surely not. I mean, surely it's not a trade secret how hockey players are paid, right?

"It's more complicated than that, but when we get suspended, they dock our pay equivalent to how many games our suspension lasts. Since we aren't making bank like the NHL, we try really fucking hard not to get suspended," Colter says.

Gavin inclines his head in a brief nod. "Well, fuck Bruce Gordon then." He lifts his beer bottle in a salute, flashing that dimple again. "May he get what's coming to him."

Colter lifts his bottle in acknowledgment, his expression dark.

I place my hand on his thigh. It's rock-hard with tension, but it doesn't show on his face. He's playing it cool, way cooler than I am, because I want to crawl across the table and slap the smile off Gavin's face. He's the reason Colter is suspended right now, and he knows it.

How can he sit here and commiserate with Colter as if he didn't orchestrate the entire thing?

Elysa deserves so much better.

CHAPTER EIGHT

Colter

"What did you think?" Leia asks, pacing around our bedroom two hours after dinner. We waited until we were sure Gavin was gone before we dipped out. I didn't want to leave Elysa alone until we were sure he wouldn't return. The motherfucker is smooth. But he's a prick.

"I think we're not talking about him tonight," I murmur, tugging her into my arms when she approaches me. She's been antsy all night. I don't think she likes Gavin much. It has nothing to do with him being a bookie, either. She has killer instincts. She has to learn to trust them.

He may act like a good guy, but they all do, right? I've seen it a thousand times. Men like Gavin are a dime a dozen. They say all the right things, smile in all the right places. But the eyes never lie. His are cold.

"Colter, we have to talk about it," Leia protests.

"No. What you have to do is take that pretty dress off so I can see what belongs to me." I run my hand down her back and then sweep my hand beneath the hem of it, gathering up the fabric as I go. "I want you naked and on your knees, pretty baby."

"Colter." Her protest comes out as a moan this time, her resolve weakening.

I palm her ass before swatting it. "Strip, Leia."

"Why don't you strip and get on your knees, Bossy?" she sasses.

I release her and step back, ripping my Polo off over my head. I keep my eyes on her while I reach for my belt. She swallows hard as I undo it with one hand, ripping it through the loops. I don't say a word as I undress, stripping off one item after another.

The pulse in her throat flutters like a hummingbird's wings.

I lower myself to my knees at her feet, staring up at her. "Is this what you want, Leia? Me worshipping at your feet?" I murmur, tugging her toward me. "Me on my knees for you, pretty baby?"

"Colter," she whispers, placing her hands on my shoulder.

"I already worship you. I'm already on my knees. You already own me, Leia." I press my forehead against her stomach, inhaling a breath. "I love you so fucking much it's driving me crazy."

A quiet sob whispers from her lips before she steps away from me. I glance up, worried as fuck I just said too much too soon, but she's already reaching for the hem of her dress. She pulls it up her body, her eyes locked on mine.

I lose the ability to breathe as she rips it off over her head, leaving her in a royal purple bra, panties, and matching garters. She sinks to her knees in front of me, so damn graceful, so damn beautiful.

"You own me too, Colter," she whispers, her eyes watery and full of emotion. "You make me feel things I never knew existed. You make me want things I never even dreamed about before you."

"Good," I rumble, running my hand down the side of her face. "I fully intend to make all of them come true."

"Oh, yeah?" She smiles, lighting up from the inside out. "All of them, huh?"

"Fuck, yeah, Trouble."

"Then maybe you should stand up," she whispers.

"Fuck," I groan. "You want my cock in your mouth, don't you?"

"Yes."

I drag her to me to kiss her long and deep. When I let her up, we're both panting for breath. I rise to my feet, stepping up in front of her. My cock is already rock hard and standing at attention, eager for the sweet torment she's about to inflict on me.

She sits forward on her knees, running one hand up my thigh. "Jesus, Colter. This thing is even more massive up close and personal," she mutters. "Why are you God's favorite? You're bossy and annoying."

"You love every inch of it," I growl, fisting my hand into her hair. "Especially when you're bouncing on it."

Her cheek brushes the head. My stomach muscles clench. Jesus. I hope she enjoys this because there's no way I have the strength to survive her doing it often. I already like that mouth too much. Having it on my cock is going to ruin me.

She blows across my shaft, and my hand tightens in her hair.

"Stop teasing and suck my cock, Trouble," I groan. It's supposed to be an order, but I think it might actually be a plea. *Have mercy on me, pretty baby. I'm just a man.*

She laughs up at me, those sky-blue eyes bright with humor. "Shush, Bossy. This is my fantasy, remember?"

"Yeah?" I press my thumb to her chin, gently forcing her mouth open. Once she's where I want her, I press the head of my cock to her lips, running it back and forth across them. "This is mine, pretty baby."

She moans softly, flicking her tongue out to taste the precum welling from the slit.

"You like that?"

"Yes."

"Good girl," I murmur. "I fucking knew you would." I slip the head past her perfect lips, growling as her hot mouth engulfs it. "Fuck. Your mouth is perfect."

She whimpers around me, her eyes dark with desire.

"Suck it, pretty baby. Take me deep." I thrust in and out of her mouth a couple of inches, showing her what to do. She doesn't need much instruction, though. She's already bobbing on my cock, eager to learn. Eager to please. God-damn. She's perfect.

I rock my hips, groaning as my dick disappears between her lips again and then again. She moans around me; her lips stretched to capacity. She can't even take half of me but tries like hell anyway.

"Look at you," I groan, holding her hair away from her face. "You look so beautiful on your knees with my cock in your mouth. You're sucking me like a goddess."

She claws at my thighs, pulling me closer.

I take control, pumping my hips in slow, steady strokes, giving us both what we want. Her eyes light up, letting me know I read her right. This is her fantasy, what she dreamed about. Me fucking her mouth, taking what I want from her.

"Mm, goddamn," I groan. "Maybe I'll just use this hot little mouth to get myself off."

She moans, desire flaring brighter in her eyes.

"That's what you want, isn't it? For me to come down this perfect throat?"

She bobs her head.

I pump my hips again, holding her on my cock for a moment before I pull back suddenly. My dick falls from her mouth. Her soft cry of disappointment ends in a gasp when I snatch her off of the floor into my arms.

"Too bad," I growl, stomping toward the bed with her. "I'm not coming anywhere except that cunt tonight, Leia."

"Colter!" She claws at my back like a little hellcat.

I toss her gently toward the bed before following her down. She lands on her stomach with me on top of her, pinning her carefully in place.

"Stay just like this," I whisper in her ear.

She moans my name as I work my way down her body, kissing everywhere I can reach. I nip at her skin, torment-ing her now. I touch and kiss and lick, teasing her into a frenzy. When she's sobbing beneath me, I rip her panties down her legs, lifting her ass into the air.

"Colter!" she screams as I lunge, attacking her with my tongue from behind. She falls forward slightly, burying her face in the pillows to muffle her cries as I gorge myself on her. Her honey floods my system, sending me reeling toward fucklust.

What is it about this woman that makes me crazy? How is it that she manages to ground me and set me ablaze at the same fucking time? I don't know, but she does. I've never felt more settled than I do with her, more at peace. And I've never felt more amped up and jittery either, like an addict needing another hit.

I press my tongue to the tight ring of muscle at her back entrance, curling my fingers up to stroke her G-spot simultaneously. She screams as she catapults over the edge, shocked and too turned on to deny she likes it. Fuck. I'm going to have so much fun with her.

Before she even has a chance to come down, I rise up behind her, notch myself at her entrance, and drive into her. She screams my name, her orgasm igniting all over again. She's so damn tight like this. Ah, God. She's killing me.

"God, Leia," I groan. "You feel like heaven, pretty baby."

"Colter, Colter," she moans in a daze.

I pound into her, fucking her hard and deep. My balls smack against her with every stroke. She pushes back against me, her ass in the air, her cheek flat against the pillows.

"I love you."

I stop moving. Stop breathing.

"I love you."

"Jesus." I flip her over, pulling her into my arms. My heart pulses with emotion, threatening to crack wide open. "Say it again, Trouble," I whisper.

"I love you, Colter."

I crush her to my chest, crush my lips to her. We touch and fuck, lost in the emotion of the moment. Lost in one another. God, I don't ever want to be found again. I want to stay like this forever, with this goddess wrapped around me, breathing life into me every time she shatters around me.

"Colter, Colter," she chants, her head thrown back and her nails in my shoulder blades as I drive her toward the edge again. "Oh, God. I can't take it anymore. It's too much."

"No," I growl, dragging my teeth down the tendon in her throat. "It's not enough. It'll never be enough, Leia." I rock her against me, reaching between us to stroke her clit. "Come for me, pretty baby. Give me one more."

"I can't!" she cries.

"You can," I breathe. "Just one more, Leia. Give me just one more."

"O-one more."

"Good girl." I grind my thumb against her clit, rocking her against me. She whines my name, unable to stop the way she moves with me, unable to keep herself from chasing the pleasure. Her head tips back, a loud cry expelling from her lips as she shatters a final time.

I drop her on me and hold her there, growling as she pulls me over with her this time. She takes everything I have, draining me dry as she shudders and shakes in my arms, glowing like the goddess she is.

When she slumps against my chest, I pull her close, holding her to my heart.

"I love you, Trouble," I breathe against her ear.

Her happy sigh is the sweetest response.

CHAPTER NINE

Leia

The next few days pass in a blur. I spend my mornings daydreaming about Colter and my nights in his bed. We don't hear anything from Gavin, but Elysa tells me he got called out of town on Saturday, so I'm not surprised.

It allows me to focus on looking into the players I know he's been in contact with. I spend most of Monday digging into Bruce Gordon and Jimmy Brinks, trying to rule out any other possible explanation, like gambling addictions. There are rumors about Bruce Gordon, but nothing I can substantiate. There's nothing on Jimmy Brinks, though. The man hasn't even been to a casino that I can find.

I leave work early on Tuesday with a headache after scouring the internet all day. Dillon calls me on the way home.

"I called your office, but Elysa said you'd already left," he says.

"Yeah, I just left a few minutes ago. What's up?"

"I've got some information on Gavin Cochran."

"What did you find?" I ask, gripping the steering wheel as a bolt of excitement shoots through me. I try shoving it back into a little box, knowing it could be nothing, but we're due for a break here.

"Have you ever heard of Dominic Grigori?"

"No?"

"Me either," Dillon mutters. "He and Gavin were partners back in NYC. Dominic was busted for insider trading a few years ago. You'll never guess why."

"Um, because he sucks?"

"Smart ass," Dillon says, making me smile. "His cousin was clerking for the Supreme Court and put a little bug in his ear on Murphy v. National Collegiate Athletic Association before the opinion was made public. He bought up a bunch of stock in companies poised to enter the sportsbook arena if a favorable decision came down from the court. Had he not bragged to the wrong person, he would have stood to make millions when their sportsbooks went live."

"Wow," I whisper. "Was Gavin involved?"

"He was never charged." Dillon hesitates. "But I looked into his fortune. He invested heavily in casinos and sportsbooks. He's taken a big hit over the last few years."

"How big?"

"One of the companies he sank a lot of money into in Jersey was raided by the government."

"So really big then," I mutter, slowing at a stop sign on Broadway.

"Yep."

"Do you think he's working with anyone?"

"He may have his buddies tied up in this, but if he does, I'm guessing he's the one pulling the strings," Dillon says. "If you ask me, I think he's looking for a surefire way to gain a foothold on sports betting. Once he irons out the kinks, he'll take it to his buddies, and they'll front the capital when he launches his own sportsbook. He'll be able to offer something his competitors can't and will sweep the board. Either that, or he'll sell the scheme to someone to recoup what he lost. Either way, he comes up smelling like roses."

"Yeah, that's what I was afraid of," I sigh. Either way, it's not good. And as of now, we have no proof that he's even committed a crime. All we have are pictures of him giving Bruce Gordon money. That's not illegal. Unless he confesses or one of the players he approaches does, we've got nothing.

"Keep me in the loop on this," Dillon says. "And don't do anything foolish, Leia. Your parents have been through enough already with Adalynn and Charlie. Don't give them another reason to worry."

"I won't, I promise."

Dillon snorts like he doesn't believe me and then disconnects.

I drop my phone in the passenger seat and head toward home, my mind racing a million miles a minute. Colter has a game tonight, and Gavin still hasn't taken our bait. At this point, I don't think he's going to take it at all. Has he already found someone on the other team to pay off?

Maybe I should be heading for the arena instead of the house. At least if he meets someone who tries to knock one of the Falcons out, we'll know that he's absolutely guilty. From there, it'll just be a matter of getting one of the guys to talk. Which one? Bruce Gordon? Jimmy Brinks? Whoever he picks tonight?

I pull up outside of the house and park, still thinking over everything. I'm halfway to the front door when my phone rings. Despite my mood, seeing Colter's name on the display brings a smile to my face.

"Hey, Bossy. You miss me already?" I ask, trying to juggle the phone and my back while unlocking the door.

"Always, Trouble." He sounds tired. Probably because he isn't getting much sleep. We're up late making love every night, and then he's up before the sun every morning to train. I don't know how he does it. "I got an interesting phone call."

"Really? So did I. You tell me yours, and I'll tell you mine." I close the front door and drop my bag by the credenza before kicking off my shoes. I'm going to get a hot shower, change, and then head to the arena. I'll camp out until the game starts and then head inside to watch Colter play.

"Gavin called," he says, his voice quiet.

I stop walking mid-step. "What? Seriously? When?"

"Ten minutes ago."

"*Why?*"

"Said he had a proposition for me."

"Holy crap. You think it's...?"

"I don't know, but he's coming to the arena," Colter growls. "Told me he'd be here around four. You think you can make it here by then?"

I pull the phone away from my ear to look at the time. It's not even two. "I can definitely be there by then. I just got home."

"What? Why?"

"My head hurts," I complain. "I spent all morning reading the internet."

"The whole internet, huh?"

"Shut up."

He chuckles. "I'm sorry you don't feel well, pretty baby. You need me to come over there and take care of you?"

"It's just a headache. I'll be fine."

"You sure?"

"Yes!" I smile, shaking my head. He's kind of adorable when he worries. "Go play with your stick or something.

I'll be there to spy on you and Gavin in about an hour. I'm going to hop in the shower first."

"Fuck," he groans. "You're getting naked and soapy without me?"

"Yep. Bye."

"I love you."

"I love you too, Bossy. Go play with your stick."

"I prefer when you do it."

"I'm hanging up now," I sing song, smiling like a crazy person. His laughter floats down the line as I end the call. Lord. He's a menace. I hope he never changes.

I send Dillon a quick text to let him know the latest, and then remember I didn't even tell Colter about my call with Dillon. It's entirely his fault for distracting me. Now, he'll just have to wait until later to hear what Dillon discovered.

Half an hour later, I've showered, changed into team colors, and am rooting around in my bag for my favorite lipstick when the front door opens.

"Colter, you crazy man," I say, not even looking up. "I told you that it's just a little headache."

He doesn't say anything.

I glance up into Gavin's gray eyes.

My heart slams against my breastbone in a jarring thud.

"G-Gavin." I lick my lips, trying to work moisture back into my mouth. "What are you doing here?"

He pushes the front door closed before stepping deeper into the living room. The fact that he isn't speaking sends chills up and down my spine. I pat around in my bag, feeling for anything I can use for a weapon. There's nothing in there that might actually hurt him, but maybe there's something that'll give me a fighting chance. Just enough of one to get away.

My phone is still in the bathroom.

My hand closes around my audio recorder.

I fumble with the buttons and hit record.

"Elysa's still at work. Did you come to pick something up for her?" I ask, playing dumb. Maybe if I act clueless, he'll think I know nothing and leave.

He flicks his gaze toward the hall.

I quickly slip my hand from the bag, dropping the audio recorder behind it on the couch.

"You've been following me," he says, his gaze drifting back to me.

"I..."

"First in your car and then in your boyfriend's truck. I knew it was you when I saw his truck out front the other night." He speaks quietly, his voice eerily calm. "Why have you been following me, Leia?"

"I..." My mind is a complete blank, panic coursing through me. "Elysa thinks you're seeing other women," I blurt the first thing that comes to mind. "She asked me to follow you to see if I caught you with anyone."

"And your boyfriend? Why was he following me?"

"He didn't know. I...I didn't want to tell him what I was doing because it sounded crazy, so he refused to leave unless I let him tag along." I shrug helplessly. "He's kind of relentless. After the grocery store, he told me that we were done following you and that you and Elysa needed to figure out your own stuff."

"Mm," Gavin says. "There's just one problem with your little story, Leia. Elysa wouldn't send you to spy on me if she thought I was seeing another woman. She'd do it herself."

Crap. He knows her better than I thought.

"You're writing a story about me, aren't you?"

"I don't know what you're talking about," I lie. "Why would I be writing a story about you?"

A sardonic smile slides across his handsome face. It's a shame he's not a very good person because he's not a bad-looking guy. He just kind of sucks as a human. "I think we both know the answer to that, don't we?"

"I wouldn't ask if I knew, Gavin." I roll my eyes. "Obviously."

"You were at the arena the night I met Bruce Gordon. Did you see me? Were you already following me, or is that what tipped you off?"

"What are you talking about?" I huff, trying to keep him talking. The more he reveals and the longer he talks, the longer I have to figure out how I'm getting out of this one. Colter is going to be pissed when he finds out Gavin came here. The sheriff isn't going to be thrilled, either. I promised I'd be careful. I should have been careful enough to lock the freaking door.

"Don't play dumb," he snaps. "It doesn't suit you."

"And doting boyfriend doesn't suit you," I mutter. "Elysa deserves so much better than you. You suck as a boyfriend, in case you didn't already know that. Your head is so far up your own butt, you need a freaking surgeon to remove it!"

"Puck bunny suits you just fine." His smile is full of venom. "You play the part of Bayliss's little whor—"

"Don't you dare," I growl, stepping toward him with my hands clenched at my sides. "Who I sleep with is *none* of your business, you disgusting creep. Why don't you stick to illegal gambling and taking out bounties on players like a good little criminal and stay out of my business?"

Triumph overtakes his expression. "Sounds like you are writing that story after all," he practically purrs. "Funny how quickly you remember details when you get angry."

Crap. I played right into his hands. He's a manipulative jerk, and I fell for the bait, exactly like he wanted. Now he knows for sure that I know. There's nothing stopping him from hurting me or, worse, killing me.

"You're going to risk their safety to line your pockets," I say, disgusted. "Do you even comprehend how vile that is, Gavin? You already have more money than you can spend in this lifetime. Do you really need more that badly?"

"It's not about money, Leia. It's about power. Others have it. I want it." He shrugs like it's simple math. "Professional sports is a billion-dollar industry. If I control the books, I control the industry."

"It still won't get you on the starting line," I point out. "That's what you really want, isn't it? To be the one wearing the jersey? To be the one idolized?" Something flickers in his eyes, and I know that's part of it. "What sport did you play, Gavin? What dream did someone crush for you?"

"Hockey," he snaps.

"So you're going to do it to others in exchange. You didn't get what you wanted, so everyone else has to pay, right? Who cares if you get some of these guys hurt or destroy their careers and futures, just so long as you get to feel like you control what happens on the ice, right?" I don't think I'm disgusted with him. I think I'm just...sad for him. That he's such a spoiled brat that he can't even see how screwed up he is. "You're like the sad little boy on the beach. The ocean knocked over your sandcastle, so now you're stomping through everyone else's. I'm not afraid of you, Gavin. I pity you."

He lunges for me like a wild animal pushed too far. I dodge him, trying to reach the front door, but he's faster than I am. He tackles me from behind, dragging us both to the floor. I land on my stomach. He falls on top of me, knocking the air out of me.

Pure terror pumps through my veins instead of blood. I don't freeze or flee. I fight. Like hell. That's who I am. That's what I do. I fight. I scratch, claw, and bite as he tries to flip me over onto my back, refusing to die easily.

A loud roar rips through the room, and then Gavin goes flying.

I stare in shock as Colter rushes past me, running right at Gavin. He falls on top of him, striking him squarely in the face.

"You sorry motherfucker!" he roars, hitting him again and then again.

"Leia." Dillon leans down over me. "Are you okay?"

"Fine. Get Colter. He's going to kill him."

Dillon nods and strides across the room. "Colter, stop. Leia needs you."

As soon as he says my name, Colter freezes with his fist raised to strike Gavin again. He whips around to face me, his face contorted with rage, his fist dotted with Gavin's blood. His eyes meet mine. He bellows like a wounded bear, throwing Gavin down.

He's across the room to me in two seconds, lifting me into his arms.

"Leia," he breathes, burying his face in my hair. "Ah, God. Leia. I'm here. I'm right here."

I cling to him, sobbing.

CHAPTER TEN

Colter

I don't let Leia out of my sight until Gavin is in the back of Dillon's SUV. I try to convince her to go to the hospital to get checked out, but she refuses. She says she's fine, but she's shaken up.

The motherfucker was on top of her, trying to get his hands around her throat when I walked in. My whole life flashed before my eyes. I don't know why I left the arena to go check on her. Something just told me that she needed me. Dillon was already in the driveway when I pulled up. He said he'd tried calling her, but she didn't answer. When he drove by and saw Gavin's car out front, he knew something was wrong.

He'd already phoned for backup. I wasn't waiting that long, though.

I'll never forget the sight of that motherfucker trying to hurt her. I'll never forget the look in her eyes. And if I live to one thousand, I'll never, ever forget that my woman is a badass. She clawed his face and arms all to hell. Took a chunk out of his arm and one of his hands too.

She also managed to record everything. Since Texas is a one-party consent state, his ass is toast. He may have gotten a slap on the wrist for illegal gambling, but he won't be so lucky regarding the home invasion and attempted murder charges.

"Wait!" Elysa cries, jumping out of her car before Dillon can pull away with him in the back. She waves her arms in the air, stepping in front of Dillon's SUV. "Wait!"

"What the fuck is she doing?" I mutter to Leia.

"I don't know." Leia steps in that direction, but I reel her back in. She's not getting anywhere near that SUV so long as he's in it.

Dillon taps the brakes, letting his window down.

"I'd like to speak to him, please," Elysa says, her voice firm. "It'll only take a minute."

"Jesus Christ," Dillon mutters, throwing the SUV in park in the middle of the road. He hops out, pulling open the back door for Elysa to speak to Gavin.

Gavin's hunched over, hiding his face. The EMTs patched him up, but his face is fucked. He probably needs to be in the hospital, but Dillon's taking his sweet time getting him there. Not that I'm complaining or anything. Let the dick suffer. It's the least he deserves.

"You're an asshole," Elysa announces. "I hope you lose everything in prison and spend the rest of your miserable life haunted by today."

He says something to her, too quietly to hear. Whatever it is doesn't seem to sway her one bit.

"Well, too bad. We're finished, Gavin. Lose my number." She turns on her heel and sashays away without looking back.

Gavin leans his head against the back of Dillon's seat. Did the jackass really think she'd stick with him after today?

Dillon shakes his head like he's asking himself the same exact question and slams the door.

"Leia!" Elysa rushes toward my woman, who steps out of my arms to meet her in one of those giant, comforting hugs girls do. The shit is cute. "I'm so glad you're okay!"

"Me too," Leia says, laying her head on Elysa's shoulder. "I'm so glad you dumped him."

"Ugh, me too. I've been waiting for days to do that!"

"What did he say to you?"

Elysa scowls. "He told me he was in love with me. As if I even care. You do not get to mess with my best friend and then say some crazy crap like that," she huffs. "He's lost his freaking mind."

Leia cracks a smile, her first in hours. The sight of it settles me. The last of the rage still coursing through my veins washes away, unable to withstand the power of that smile. She's right here, safe and happy. The rest will work itself out.

"Remind me not to take story ideas from Elysa ever again," she says hours later, groaning as she falls backward onto our bed. "I'm so tired and haven't even started writing yet."

"It's been a helluva day, Trouble." I dim the lights before scooping her up to strip her down. Once she's naked, I slide the covers back and deposit her in bed. We've been at the Sheriff's Department for hours. I end up missing the game, but I don't fucking care. I don't think anyone else did either once they discovered what happened.

Coach has already been on the phone with the bigwigs of the League, letting them know the situation. I'm guessing Jimmy Brinks and Bruce Gordon will have bad days soon. I'd feel sorry for them, except they made their own choices, knowing full well the risks they took. If they were dumb enough to do the crime, they can suck it up and do the time.

I don't know if they'll be banned from the league, but I doubt they'll be on the ice for the rest of the season. It's almost a shame, really. I was looking forward to kicking the shit out of Gordon at the next game. After all this, I doubt anyone would even blame me.

"Mmhmm," she mumbles, stealing my pillow to snuggle up with it while I undress. "Can we stick to boring for a while, Bossy? I'm all adventured out."

"Whatever you want, pretty baby," I agree, knowing damn well she'll change her mind in the morning. Leia wouldn't know what to do with boredom. She was born for adventure and excitement. It's part of who she is, just like that smart mouth and her fiery spirit. She told me the other day that her adopted mom picked her name. She chose well.

"Your brother hates me." I crawl into bed with her, stealing my pillow back as I pull her onto my chest. All of her family in town met us at the Sheriff's Department. I guess Dillon called to let them know what happened. Her sisters are sweet. But her brother, Garrett? He did not seem thrilled that she was dating me.

She laughs quietly. "Garrett hates everyone with a penis who even looks at us."

"Fuck my life."

"He likes hockey, so you'll probably get off easy." She laughs again. "Razor was in a rock band. Garrett still thinks he's up to no good, and he and Adalynn are married and have a baby on the way."

"Jesus, Trouble. You aren't making me feel any better here," I mutter.

She pats my chest. "You'll be fine. Just talk about sports. And avoid mentioning the fact that you've seen me naked. He might shoot you if you tell him that."

"You little minx." I dig my fingers into her sides, making her squeal with laughter. "You're fucking with me again."

"Only a little bit," she promises, swatting my hands away. "Garrett's just grumpy. He's hiding something, but we don't know what. He's like Fort Knox."

"He's in love."

"Really?" She blinks up at me. "You think so?"

"I know so, pretty baby. I can read the signs." I tuck a strand of hair behind her ear. "I see the same ones in the mirror every day."

Her expression softens. "You're awfully good at that."

"Yeah?" I tilt her chin up to brush my lips across hers. "Good enough for you to spend the rest of your life with me?"

"Colter," she gasps. "Are you—?"

"Asking you to marry me? Damn right." I grab my wallet from the nightstand and pull her ring out. I hid it in there since she likes to snoop. I didn't want her to find it before I could give it to her.

She stops breathing when I slip it onto her finger.

"Marry me, goddess," I whisper, bringing her hand up to press my lips to the solitaire diamond. "Let me spend the rest of my life loving you."

"Will there be excitement?" she asks.

"You are the excitement."

"What about adventure?"

"Every fucking day."

"In that case, I need to think about it."

I growl, tipping her over beneath me.

"I'm kidding! I'm kidding!" she squeals, flinging her arms around my neck. "Yes, Colter. Of course, my answer is yes."

"It damn well better be," I mutter, my lips hovering over hers. "You're stuck with me, Trouble. Permanently."

"Oh, yeah?" She slides her hands down my shoulders, smirking. "Does that mean I get to do what I want to do to you then?"

"Nope. It means I get to have my way with you." I cut her off her protest with my lips on hers. When I let her up for air, she isn't protesting anymore. In fact, she doesn't protest for a long, long time.

EPILOGUE

Leia

Five Years Later

"I need your help with a story."

"Hell no," Colter growls, spinning around at the kitchen sink to face me.

I take one look at his expression and crack up. "You look like you'd rather walk across glass barefoot."

"Is that an option? If so, I'm taking it."

"Chicken."

He tosses the dish towel at me, smirking. "Call me what you want, pretty baby. Every damn time I help you, it ends up being some dangerous bullshit that I live to regret. So hell no, I'm not helping you with whatever it is. And you aren't looking into it either. Give it to someone who doesn't have my baby cooking."

"Spoilsport." I stick my tongue out at him, patting my belly. I'll never admit it, but he's probably right. Every time I ask for his help, one of us ends up in danger. It's exhausting, honestly. Millionaires and billionaires have a lot of skeletons in their closets. I should probably stop looking for them, but I can't seem to help myself.

If there's a mystery to solve, I naturally want to solve it. It's what I'm good at. I never thought I'd love that part of my job the most, but I do. Even when it's dangerous.

Colter will never admit it, but he loves helping me just as much. We've been a team for five years. He always has my back. It doesn't matter what the story is; I can always count on him to help me figure it out or do something crazy to get the information I need. He's Superman as far as I'm concerned.

He retired from the AHL last year. He coaches at the college level in Houston now. He loves it. He especially loves spending more time at home with me and our two boys. Our youngest, Sutter, may take after his daddy. But our oldest, Drake, has no interest in sports. That may change one day, but we're not pushing either of them toward hockey or any other sport. The choice should be theirs.

The same goes for our daughter when she gets here in a few months. They have a whole world of possibilities. We want them to chase whatever dreams they have, not try to cram themselves into the dreams we make for them.

So long as they're happy and healthy, we're happy. And we *are* happy. Every day with Colter is an adventure. And every night is a dream come true. I never imagined this was what the future held for me when I stepped into that locker room five years ago. I couldn't have imagined it. But, God, I'm so freaking glad I got lost.

I found nirvana, and it's beautiful.

"What's the story?" Colter asks, pulling me into his arms.

"The perfume guy who lives in town just announced his plan to sell his wife's company for billions," I murmur. "Less than two months after his missing daughter was legally declared dead."

"Shit. You think he killed his own daughter?"

"Her shares passed to him when she died, making him the majority stakeholder. But he was allegedly in France when she went missing."

"How long has she been missing?"

"Since a few weeks after her eighteenth birthday."

"Jesus," he mutters, dropping his head to mine. "You aren't going to be able to let this go, are you?"

"She's been missing for seven years," I whisper. "If he didn't kill her, where is she?"

Colter sighs heavily. "I guess we'll find out one way or another, pretty baby. But don't even fucking think about putting yourself or my baby in danger, do you hear me?" He tips my chin up, his gaze unyielding. "I will spank your gorgeous ass until you plead for mercy if the thought even crosses your mind."

"You know I wouldn't do that." I place a hand on my belly, cradling my bump.

"I know, but you couldn't stay out of trouble if I paid you, pretty baby." He shakes his head, his expression rueful. "You attract it like a damn magnet."

"I do not."

"Yeah, you do." He tips my head back, brushing his lips across mine. "How the fuck do you think you ended up married to me, goddess?"

"Good point. Maybe I should see if it's too late to trade you in on a less troublesome model," I mutter, turning on my heel as if I'm going to leave the kitchen.

He grabs me, pulling me back into his arms. Before I can protest, he scoops me up into his arms and strides out of the kitchen.

"Where are we going?"

"Gonna remind you why you like this troublesome model so much," he growls, heading for the stairs.

"The boys will be home in half an hour."

"Then it's a good thing I can make you come in five, isn't it?"

"I guess so." I smile, pressing my face to his shoulder. God, I love him. He promised me a life of excitement and adventure, and he delivered. Every single day with him just gets better and better. I have a feeling they always will. He'll make sure of it.

AUTHOR'S NOTE

Thanks so much for reading Leia and Colter's story! If you enjoyed it, please consider leaving a review! Noah's story and Atlas's storyare now available!

SILVER SPOON FALCONS

What we wanted: professional athletes. What we got: stick-wielding madmen who look good in blue, play hard, and love harder. It's a good thing this is Silver Spoon Falls because these hunky hockey players fit right in.

Welcome the Falcons to the roster! These over-the-top athletes are about to play the most important game of all: the game of love. And the sassy, curvy women of Silver Spoon Falls have no intention of going down without a fight.

Let the games begin!

Check out the series: https://www.amazon.com/dp/B0C6KGFG8H

- Allie's Enforcer by Loni Ree (June) - https://www.amazon.com/gp/product/B0B9HY6GJJ

- Leia's Playmaker by Nichole Rose (July) - https://mybook.to/LeiaFalcons

- Carlie's Coach by Loni Ree (August) - https://www.amazon.com/gp/product/B0BRYMJGRL

- Aspen's Defense by Nichole Rose (September) - https://mybook.to/AspensDefense

- Lana's Winger by Lonie Ree (October) - https://www.amazon.com/gp/product/B0BRYM4YFZ

- Gabbi's Goalie by Nichole Rose (November) - https://mybook.to/GabbisGoalie

ICE STORM

A secret relationship with his best friend's baby sister? This hockey star may be in over his head.

Kellan

No one walks through the doors of *Dionysus* unless they're on a mission.

It's a hedonistic paradise.

But when my teammate asks me to help him find his baby sister inside, I agree anyway.

Parker is new in town and doesn't know what she's getting herself into.

Apparently, neither do I.

One look at the curvy little princess, and the last thing on my mind is getting her out of the club.

When she asks me to teach her what she's aching to learn, I know I shouldn't agree with her insane proposition.

But I'll do anything to keep her close...even if it means letting her believe I'm playing by her rules.

Keeping our relationship hidden from her brother is a bad idea, but I'm in too deep now.

When he finds out the truth, it may just tear our whole team apart.

Parker

I don't know why I went to Dionysus.

Or how I found myself in a private room upstairs.

But the second Kellan walks in, I know I want to stay.

Something about him makes me ache to obey his every little command.

But he's my brother's teammate, and this has bad idea written all over it.

That doesn't stop me from propositioning him.

It doesn't stop him from agreeing, either.

Now, I'm in serious trouble.

I swore I wouldn't fall for him, but my heart refuses to listen.

When my brother finds out, he's going to lose his mind.

I don't want to be the reason his team loses the Cup and their friendship ends...but I can't lose Kellan, either.

What am I supposed to do?

Ice Storm is out now.

INSTALOVE BOOK CLUB

The Instalove Book Club is now in session!

Get the inside scoop from your favorite instalove authors, meet new authors to love, and snag a free book and bonus content from featured authors every month. The Instalove Book Club newsletter goes out once per week!

Join the Club: http://instalovebookclub.com

NICHOLE'S BOOK BEAUTIES

Want to connect with Nichole and other readers? We're building a girl gang! Join Nichole Rose's Book Beauties on Facebook for fun, games, and behind-the-scenes exclusives!

FOLLOW NICHOLE

Like free books? Me too! Sign-up for my mailing list at http://authornicholerose.com/newsletter to stay up-to-date on all new releases and for exclusive giveaways and freebies!

Want to connect with me and other readers? Join Nichole Rose's Book Beauties on Facebook!

facebook.com/AuthorNicholeRose/

instagram.com/AuthorNicholeRose

twitter.com/AuthNicholeRose

bookbub.com/authors/nichole-rose

tiktok.com/@authornicholerose

ALSO BY NICHOLE ROSE

<u>Her Alpha Series</u>

Her Alpha Daddy Next Door

Her Alpha Boss Undercover

Her Alpha's Secret Baby

Her Alpha Protector

Her Date with an Alpha

Her Alpha: The Complete Series

<u>Her Bride Series</u>

His Future Bride

His Stolen Bride

His Secret Bride

His Curvy Bride

His Captive Bride

His Blushing Bride

His Bride: The Complete Series

Claimed Series
Possessing Liberty

Teaching Rowan

Claiming Caroline

Kissing Kennedy

Claimed: The Complete Series

Love on the Clock Series
Adore You

Hold You

Keep You

Protect You

Love on the Clock: The Complete Series

The Billionaires' Club
The Billionaire's Big Bold Weakness

The Billionaire's Big Bold Wish

The Billionaire's Big Bold Woman

The Billionaire's Big Bold Wonder

The Billionaires' Club: The Complete Series

Playing for Keeps
Cutie Pie

Ice Breaker

Ice Prince

Ice Giant

Cold as Ice

Ice Storm

Full-Length Titles

Crash into You

Fight for You (coming soon)

Kill for You (coming soon)

The Second Generation

A Blushing Bride for Christmas

Love Bites

Come Undone

Dripping Pearls

Echoes of Forever

His Christmas Miracle

Taken by the Hitman

Wicked Saint

The Ruined Trilogy

Physical Science

Wrecked

Wanton

Wicked

Ruined: The Complete Series

Illicit Love Series

Irresistible

Irrevocable

Irreplaceable

Irredeemable

Destination Romance

Romancing the Cowboy

Beach House Beauty

Standalone Titles

A Touch of Summer

Black Velvet

His Secret Obsession

Dirty Boy

Naughty Little Elf

Tempted by December

Devil's Deceit
A Bride for the Beast (writing with Fern Fraser)
A Hero for Her
Pretty Little Mess
Dear Mr. Dad Bod

<u>Easy on Me</u>
Easy Ride
Easy Surrender

<u>One Night with You</u>
Falling Hard
Model Behavior
Learning Curve
Angel Kisses

<u>Silver Spoon MC</u>
The Surgeon
The Heir
The Lawyer
The Prodigy
The Bodyguard
Silver Spoon MC Collection: Nichole's Crew

<u>Silver Spoon Falls</u>

Xavier's Kitten

Callum's Hope

Snow's Prince

Aurora's Knight

<u>Silver Spoon Falcons</u>

Leia's Playmaker

Aspen's Defense (coming soon)

Gabbi's Goalie (coming soon)

<u>writing with Loni Ree as Loni Nichole</u>

Dillon's Heart

Razor's Flame

Ryker's Reward

Zane's Rebel

Oral Arguments

Grizz's Passion

Garrett's Obsession

About Nichole Rose

Nichole Rose writes filthy romance for curvy readers. Her books feature headstrong, sassy women and the alpha males who consume them. From grumpy detectives to country boys with attitude to instalove and over-the-top declarations, nothing is off-limits.

Nichole is sure to have a steamy, sweet story just right for everyone. She fully believes the world is ugly enough without trying to fit falling in love into a one-size-fits-all box.

When not writing, Nichole enjoys fine wine, cute shoes, and everything supernatural. She is happily married to the love of her life and is a proud mama to the world's most ridiculous fur-babies. She and her husband live in Arkansas.

You can learn more about Nichole and her books at authornicholerose.com.

facebook.com/AuthorNicholeRose/

instagram.com/AuthorNicholeRose

twitter.com/AuthNicholeRose

bookbub.com/authors/nichole-rose

tiktok.com/@authornicholerose